Grass Heart

Grass Heart

M. M. B. Walsh

✦

Afterword by James Colbert

UNIVERSITY OF NEW MEXICO PRESS

ALBUQUERQUE

Library of Congress Cataloging-in-Publication Data

Walsh, M. M. B.
Grass heart / M. M. B. Walsh ; introduction by
James Colbert.— 1st ed.
p. cm.
ISBN 0-8263-2338-3 (alk. paper)
1. Mandan Indians—Fiction. 2. Great Plains—Fiction.
3. Smallpox—Fiction. I. Title.
PS3573.A4722 G7 2001
813'.54—dc21
2001001512

Book design: Mina Yamashita

Grass Heart

On the high prairie beyond the village, wolves and coyotes raised their quarrelsome songs as a quarter moon appeared among the flying stars above the treetops, and Jake Moon sighed with happiness. It was a night such as he had dreamed of, and all that he expected from his dreams was there: the broad river, the great woods banding it, a sky resplendent with beauty, and a girl, her hand in his as they walked the path next to the river. He was pleasantly aware of the damp mossy smell rising from the water, the hushed greenness of the twilight broken by the sonorous crickets, and the curled fingers in his palm, long and narrow and of a remarkable shade. The knowledge of their strength lay well hidden in a warm softness, and there was nothing to indicate it would be the only time he would hold that hand in his with lascivious intentions swirling through his head, since those were what he entertained but never found the opportunity to act upon, not then nor later.

Sounds from the trader's fort across the water came faintly to his ears: drums and songs where the Indians were dancing, the loud shouts and laughter of the white men watching, and the calls, shrill and fixed, of guards as they walked the parapet in the early dusk.

Jake gave a small hop, as he was wont to do, having but eighteen years and not yet cemented into manhood, delighted beyond measure that he had come at last to the unknown, mysterious West, following the footsteps of Lewis and Clark, and those of his father who had traveled with them, and proud he had exceeded those of his sire who had turned back early and had made but half the distance of his son. And when Jake had grown old, and nostalgia warmed his thin blood, he took to reading all the available records of the expedition and learned his father had lied, for there was no mention of his name anywhere among them. But by then it mattered not at all; the old man was long since dead and Jake had learned the importance of such lies. He too had been guilty of such deceits, with more variety and effect.

The girl he led so gently was taller than he, a full foot longer in length, so that she was made to bend her knees when passing under low-hanging branches, the motion placing her face on the same level as his, and he was subtly conscious of how often she watched him from the low angle of her eyes, and feared she suspected his designs, although she gave no indications of it but for smiling more than once behind her other hand.

Her amusement embarrassed him; he knew how strange he must look to her, being round-bodied, with a round head he attempted to disguise by a high crowned hat he wore pulled down over his forehead and ears. He could do little to change his short stature, even by stuffing his boots with extra stockings and practicing painful stretching exercises in secret.

It was his bright blue eyes that caused Grass Heart to steal sly glances into his shadowed face. She ignored the rest of his appearance, paying little attention to it for she was not particularly attracted to white men, having known many during her short life: friends of her father, trappers and traders, and the occasional traveler who found his way upriver with no certain destination in mind. From these she had learned to speak their language, fluently, but this was the first time she had been alone with one and was overcome with an unnatural shyness alien to her nature.

The two had not spoken for some time, until a wild dove was disturbed in her nest and questioned their passing. Jake Moon stopped abruptly.

"That's a tasty bird," he said. "I've eaten many a one baked in mud in a fire. The feathers peel off then. I don't care one bit, though, to eat their heads like some people. Suck out their brains," and he made a slurping sound with his lips.

Grass Heart straightened her legs so suddenly her head vanished in the leaves and he was alarmed at its disappearance. Her voice came down to him, filled with steel, sharp as a good knife blade.

"We never kill them. They are medicine birds. It brings bad luck."

Jake considered that a foolish notion and told her so, while standing tiptoe to free her hair. It was crowned with twigs where she had thrashed about, and when at last she stood out from under the offending branch she loosed on him a fierce glare.

"Well, I didn't intend to make you mad," he said, aggrieved, and put his arms around her waist. "You are sure pretty," he murmured.

"I am handsome," she replied, shrugging him off. "My father says so, and I respect his judgment."

Jake had heard of her father when he first arrived at the fort. There had been talk of how rich Good Plume was, how he owned an enormous horse herd, what a shrewd trader he had been in the earlier days before he grew old, getting the best price for his furs. He dressed his only child in the finest clothing, and Jake could believe it, looking at her, her dress heavily beaded with extra fringes, and silver hoops in her ears. Around her throat hung beads of turquoise, and garnets, and long necklaces of rare shells. And she was given a freedom seldom found in girls of her age, which was why Jake had chosen her to walk with him that night. He thought perhaps it had something to do with her size, for he had felt the sleek muscles along her back and arms when he held her. He thought her magnificent. After he knew her better he often mused on what a splendid warrior she would have made.

They resumed walking, this time at a faster pace. The shadows had deepened, and nighthawks skimmed the trees, their plaintive cries piercing the darkness. Grass Heart turned away from the river into deeper forest, and Jake felt a stir of anticipation that reached to the soles of his feet and made them tingle. It was quieter but for the scuttling of small unseen animals and the mutter of a bird nearby. The path narrowed and Grass Heart walked before him. He peered at the steady rolling of her haunches under the doeskin skirt, idly wondering if it was possible to seduce her with sweet talk and discarding the idea almost before it had formed itself fully. Her rebuff, when he had clutched her earlier, had given him little encouragement, and it seemed only his original plan would work: luring her far enough from her village so that when he tripped her and fell on top of her when she hit the ground whatever noise she raised would go unheard.

Once he had her in that position, he was willing to take his chances.

When he had encircled her waist he found no knife concealed there, but he knew that was no guarantee one was not hidden somewhere on her person. He also took into account she might be wearing a protective band around her upper thighs; Indian girls often employed them against rape. It made him giddy to think of what lay before him and stepped up his pace to match hers.

In a clearing in the trees he made ready to jump her from behind, when suddenly she stopped. He bumped into her. There was just enough light for him to see the form of an Indian leaning against a tree. He wore a blanket and from its folds came a soft giggle.

Envy dried his mouth. Dear God, he sighed inwardly, how easy these fellows have it. Easy girls. Easy living. Plenty of horses, good hunting all summer, a warm lodge when the snow came. As many wives as a man could handle, too!

You told them: Dress out those furs; bring me my pipe and tobacco; cook the meat. *Come to my bed.* What more could a man want in this world? It formed in his mind first as a seed, thrust up a stalk, burst into bloom, all in an instant, and he nearly swooned.

I could have it all if I married Grass Heart.

Dazed, he grasped her by the arm. She hissed at him, wriggling away. "Let go, I want to see who is in that blanket."

"Come on," he said urgently, "it's just some girl. I've got to talk to you now!" He took her firmly by both arms and pushed her along the path. A shaft of moonlight fell between the trees and into his eyes. Their shine, bright and piercing, mellowed her rising temper, and she allowed him to lead her to a fallen tree where they sat down. She fiddled with her skirt, her long legs splayed out before her, and tried to see the embroidery on her moccasins.

Jake debated whether or not to get to his knees, but decided against it and took her hand in his.

"I want you for my wife," he said.

Grass Heart fought off a sudden evil urge to laugh and stared at her unseen feet.

"I want to marry you," said Jake, "and make you my wife. I am in love with you."

She put one shell from one of her necklaces in her mouth and ran her tongue over it. It was cool and tasted slightly of salt.

"Don't give me any answer now. Think it over," he said, still in that slow urgent voice, and reached under his coat. He brought out a brown paper parcel. "A token of my affection," Jake whispered, and put it in her hands. "Kiss me."

"Bloody Christ," she said. "I don't want to kiss you and I don't want to marry you."

⏤

IN HER ELEVENTH YEAR, two years before she met Jake Moon, Grass Heart had fallen in love with a youth several years her senior. His name was Bloody Dog. She followed him everywhere, with total, single-minded devotion that consumed her days and disturbed her sleep. He found it impossible to discourage her; she pursued him relentlessly.

"Let me ride with you," she begged, and he kicked his pony with such vigor the animal almost threw him, sweeping off onto the prairie in a rush of wind and dust.

"Let me walk with you," she pleaded, and his friends whistled and jeered as she put her moccasins in his tracks, making them hers.

"Don't do this," he told her nicely. "You are a nuisance. I can't have a child on my heels."

"I am not a child. I could walk beside you if you didn't hurry so," she said to him. "I think it is time we got married. We should do it right away before we get too old." Her face was moist with earnestness and sweat.

"I want you to go home," he ordered, raising his voice. It cracked on the final word, and he felt his cheeks grow warm with embarrassment. "Go," he said.

"You love me too," she said tenderly, "I can see it on your face. You think of me all the time. We'll marry and have children."

He groaned loudly. "Go away. You are but a child yourself. I don't even like you."

"We'll marry, all right," and she stamped her foot, raising puffs of dirt. "God Almighty, don't you see it's going to happen?"

Nothing deterred her; she continued to pursue him. He found himself plotting how to escape her, and began riding out with his uncle every day, a wise, modest man who was glad to have him along, and who watched with benign amusement the fury of the little girl who stood at the corral fence yelling when Bloody Dog brought out his pony.

"That one is a devil," he remarked to his nephew. "She will catch you yet."

Grass Heart attempted to follow on her old fat mare. No matter how hard she beat it, she always failed.

She nagged her father to give her a faster horse, and he agreed, but only after obtaining her promise she would not ride it out of sight of the village. Because he set a watch on her she was made to oblige him, and the old warrior he hired reported that she rode just on the horizon, that he could see her head and upper torso bobbing along the skyline. She soon tired of this aimless riding and left her new pony in the corral and sat outside the village in a high tree, scanning the prairie for Bloody Dog's return.

The contest between the girl and the youth was a matter of gossip in the village, and bets were laid on the outcome. Good Plume stayed in his lodge, sharpening arrow heads, his humiliation affecting his touch so that he ruined more than he completed.

His sister Least Mouse came, unwanted, to talk to him of his daughter's behavior, and he told her, "Mind your own business. I can handle her. You worry over your own girls."

Least Mouse bridled. Her own four daughters were mean-minded, sly as weasels, and fought among themselves. They were greedy and ate competitively, and their skin was pebbled with ugly sores, their eyes clouded with despair.

"Don't come to me for advice when she disgraces herself," she said, sniffing noisily.

For Bloody Dog, the unequal struggle was distressing enough without the peculiar desires he had begun to feel. It puzzled him that he felt no interest in girls; rather he preferred the company of his own sex and sought out young warriors, drawn to them by their singular masculinity. And when he could no longer suppress his instincts, he went in dismay to his uncle, beseeching him to build him a sweat lodge so that he could seek some vision that might give him a solution to his problem.

"I will build the lodge," Long Catcher said, "and perhaps you will receive whatever you are looking for, but can't we talk of it first?"

"I can't," Bloody Dog replied, his face hot with shame.

"Whatever is troubling you will go away in time, even that girl who chases you." Long Catcher loved the boy as though he were his own; he had been given to him to care for, to instruct in matters of the hunt, and war, and to guide his heart, as was the custom in their village. He remembered with sadness how the youth in childhood had hung back when his companions played at mock war with spears; and the doll he had had, a poor thing his sister had discarded, and the attention Bloody Dog had lavished on it until made to throw it away as unseemly, a girl's toy.

Long Catcher carefully scanned the youth's face, the expression on it pained at the moment. The nose was arched but had no fierceness in its curve. It rose to a brow delicate as a girl's, below which were eyes lashed like mink fur, and a jaw too gentle to hold a man's mouth.

"We can speak of anything, the two of us." And Long Catcher drew him down on the mat and waited.

It was a long time before Bloody Dog spoke, and then he mumbled so that his uncle had to prod him to speak louder. "I don't like girls," he said and hid his head in his arms.

"Ah," sighed Long Catcher in pity.

"I only like men."

The uncle searched in his pocket for a bit of sweet bark gum and chewed on it absently. Deep thought was alien to him; his duty to this boy made him try. His brow pleated, he beat on the side of his head with a fist. Nothing came but a thought, stealthy as a thief from a hidden cave: I will be blamed for this.

"I think I know the answer," he announced, "yes, I think I know what is wrong."

That done, he tried again, this time slapping his cheek with his hand. His nose began to bleed, just enough that he had to stop to wipe it away. His bloody palm drew his eyes downward and he looked awhile at the red stain.

"Yes." His voice gained power. "It is the way you were made. I believe your blood runs in a different direction than mine. I think it moves backwards through your body. It may even be," he continued, "that your heart was made on the wrong side. If that is so, there is nothing you can do but to love men."

Bloody Dog sat, chin in hand. To him it sounded very reasonable; his blood ran another way because his heart was in the wrong place. Relief cooled his brow and stopped up the flow of sweat from under his arms. He wondered what evil spell had been laid on his mother before his birth, or what bad spirit had crept into the lodge, laying its hand on her swollen belly as he slept within her, causing his heart to shift itself and his blood to run in another direction.

He thanked Long Catcher and ran home, light of foot, and light of heart, wherever it lay. In the morning he put on one of his sister's gowns and walked around the lodge, excited with the freedom it gave. He experimented with his hair, unbraiding it. It fell in loose waves almost to his waist. Adding a few simple ornaments he went to his father's polished shield and looked at himself, pleased with what he saw. Then, as his mother looked on in bewilderment and his sister wept at his strangeness, he added a string of blue beads and a bracelet and walked out of the lodge.

At first no one knew him, and when they did recognize him their eyes showed varying degrees of shock. In Long Catcher's lodge, while his aunt regarded him, a baffled shine to her stare, his uncle merely raised his heavy eyebrows.

"One cannot argue with blood," he told Bloody Dog. In the council lodge that night he let it be known that he had diagnosed a difficult case and was seriously considering taking up medicine, bringing a respectful silence from all but the regular medicine men, who hooted loudly at the notion.

The elders went to Bloody Dog's parents and told them he must take a new name. His uncle held a naming feast, and after eating, a sing was held, to which the women were invited.

He was now Sweet Flag, and among the people there was a general acceptance of his new status. He had become a berdache. At first his flirting was awkward indeed, but he soon became adept with the turkey wing, brushing it across his face, and it wasn't long before he did it as gracefully as the most accomplished woman. He had new clothing, elegant dresses with elegant beadwork. And he found a protector, a man he fancied, one who saved him from the old men who tried to drag him into the bushes outside the gates. He lived in his own small lodge, on the far side of the village, and entertained with style.

When Grass Heart learned all this, she raged and screamed and cried incessantly. Nothing soothed her. She grew listless and complained her heart pained her, and Good Plume feared for her life.

One day she ventured out of the lodge and met Sweet Flag face to face, and he spoke first, saying, "We can still be friends." His smile was soft and shy.

"Never!" she cried passionately. "Look at you! I have plenty of girl friends and don't want another."

"It's in my blood," he explained, retreating a few steps. "And my heart—I can't change either one, it was the way I was made."

At that her demeanor changed: her shoulders fell downwards, her spine curved with dismay, and the little flaw in her eye seemed to dim and lose its edges. "I love you," she said. "I'll always love you," and she hooked her thumbs in her belt and forced herself to stand straight while she looked him up and down, slowly and with a curious deliberation.

"What a waste," she murmured. "A bloody waste."

A long time passed before she spoke to him again.

⮌

JAKE MOON LEANED TOWARD HER. "You could learn to love me, I just know it." She shook her head in annoyance. "I'll speak to your papa," he said.

She could either lose him in the woods or take him home to meet her father, and she decided on the latter. He'd make short work of this white man; it would make good fun to watch.

She set a swift pace that he was hard pressed to match, and he was panting before they reached the low hill where the village stood. He asked her humbly to let him rest a moment before climbing the path to the palisade, and she waited, whistling between her teeth in impatience. His face was scarlet; sweat ran warm-fingered down his spine.

Breathing more evenly, he followed her through the streets to her lodge. A pine knot flared beside the porch. Three horses stood at a rack nearby, flicking ragged tails indolently, catching a mosquito or two from among the hundreds on their haunches. Grass Heart walked around them, looking at each one, then smoothed her hair and straightened her dress.

A curtain was drawn back inside the round-topped porch to let the evening air sweeten the lodge, and bending her head the girl stepped into the room. An old woman leaned against the wall, half hidden in shadows, humming tunelessly. She held a knobbed stick in her hand, and after throwing a feeble kick at Grass Heart, which missed, she swung the stick at her legs.

Grass Heart leaped nimbly to one side. "Watch out, or I will beat the shit out of you," she said. Jake Moon was shocked. "That's only Tall Hair," she explained to him. "She's a slave. Good Plume took her from the Blood Indians when I was small. She's not worth feeding. Worms got into her head one time and make her act crazy."

He stared at the room before him. It was enormous, lit by torches that didn't reach into the darkness beneath the domed roof, far above and lost to sight. Uneasily he felt the weight of all that earth pressing down over his head; the great arch of packed dirt seemed to drone, menacingly, and he laid his back against one of the huge posts that supported it and refused to look upward again.

To his right the dim figures of horses moved in a pen, and a fat bitch with pups stirred near his feet, snarling at his strange smell. He studied her teeth before daring to look away.

Grass Heart told him to stay where he was and left him to walk to the rear of the lodge. As she stepped beyond the fire pit where a kettle steamed, he could see her no longer, and a prickle of fear trembled the inside of his wrists and thighs.

She was annoyed to see the white men sitting with Good Plume, and hesitated by the fire, where she peered into the pot boiling there. They have spoiled everything, she thought, and regretted bringing Jake Moon there. At least she had made him almost run to keep up with her, his short legs pumping madly to keep up with her longer stride. She smiled to herself secretly before turning to face the white men, whose solemn faces staring at her reminded her of three moons set on a hill.

The agent from the fort across the river grew dizzy as her long shadow fell across him. Her father cleared his throat. "Sit down," he told her, point-ing to a back rest, knowing instantly from her manner that she would cause trouble if given a chance, and sent her a warning look. Her strong white teeth shone in a malicious smile. "Mr. Knipp has brought this man to meet you," said Good Plume, after the agent introduced the man sit-ting next to him as Mr. Carl Bessie. "He is an artist," Mr. Knipp said, "and he would like to paint your portrait."

The words came out with only a slight slurring of the S's, and rather pleased with himself, Mr. Knipp sat back, his hands folded across his vest.

Boldly, Grass Heart inspected the new white man. He was overfat, like Jake Moon, but his face was private, not open, and she thought he was probably inclined to be lethargic in thought and act, unlike the agent, who drank too much and was apt to become highly emo-tional for no reason.

The third man was Mr. Childs. He sat with his head bowed over a large black book he held in his lap. He gave her a stingy nod, and in the firelight she saw the sores dappling his cheeks and chin, pustules with a peculiar glow, and turned away in disgust.

Grass Heart intended to give a quick assent to the artist's wish and rid herself of their presence, but her father forestalled her by turning to Mr. Knipp to speak of matters she had no interest in. Carl Bessie watched her idly; he was in a bad humor and had not wanted to come that evening. His stomach was upset again, and his horse had nipped his shoulder when he went to mount, tearing his good cambric shirt.

And he was disgruntled with Mr. Knipp's behavior, the result of an afternoon spent with a brandy bottle he had not been asked to share. He wished he had remained in his room at the fort, cleaning his brushes and setting his portfolio in order, but the agent had burst in and literally dragged him from it by the arm, to cross the river for a visit to the village.

Knipp, lavishing fumes in his face, had told him of a girl who was worthwhile painting, and babbled on about her father, a chief of high standing, Bessie gathered, whose cooperation the agent depended upon in his fur trade. "She's not another She Sleeps?" the artist had asked in a dry voice, recalling the last girl he had recommended, and who had caused no end of difficulties, accusing him of stealing her spirit and putting it in the picture.

They had met the man called Childs at the riverbank where it was easy to ford the waters; now it was late summer and the water ran slow in the shallows. Knipp had greeted him with a wild shout and insisted he accompany them, commandeering a horse for him from one of the hunters who came by at that moment. Carl Bessie paid little mind to the man, conscious only that he was dressed entirely in black, his face shadowed by a broad-brimmed hat. Instead, he was attentive to the splendor of the evening, with its clear light and muted sky. He tended to confuse distances in this country, and they arrived at the village sooner than he expected.

Bessie caught fragments of the conversation between the agent and the black-clad man and learned to his surprise that Childs was a preacher of sorts. Knowing Knipp had no use for religion of any kind, he blamed the brandy for his genial invitation, understanding how liquor opened reservoirs of generosity in most men.

Later he learned more about Childs, that his calling was the result of his firm and eloquent vision of evil in the world, and that his specialty was fornication. Mr. Knipp said he had an extensive knowledge of his subject and dwelt overmuch on it, to the agent's delight. Knipp also added he enjoyed greatly listening to the preacher when he spoke of it, but not otherwise.

While they were tying their horses to the rack by the lodge, Knipp had sidled up to Bessie and whispered, "I don't trust that fellow," and pointed out the shoes on the preacher's feet. "Store bought," he said triumphantly, leaving Bessie standing with his mouth agape.

He had been further startled when Good Plume came to welcome them. The Indian was extremely tall, with a curiously shaped head, elongated, narrow of skull, with flattened sides. He wore a fringe of white hair low over his eyes, reminding Bessie of snow on a headstone in a graveyard.

They went indoors, where Childs proved an embarrassment to the others for his lack of good manners. He stared in disdain at the appointments of the lodge, and they averted their faces and sat where indicated, hearing his snorts of disapproval. Knipp talked with Good Plume, Childs falling silent; instead, he scratched at his crotch and fingered the Bible he brought out of his coat.

At last the daughter came in, followed by a stout young man Bessie remembered seeing around the fort. She stopped to look in the cooking pot, and Bessie's stomach turned over with an alarming slap. It had come to him that they would be asked to eat; the stew was sure to be boiled dog. He thought he might faint and groaned aloud, so that all heads swiveled in his direction, Knipp coughing to cover his confusion at the noise.

"Your daughter is beautiful," he told Good Plume, to which she said she wasn't beautiful but handsome. Childs threw back his head, his big-brimmed hat tilting dangerously, and cried: "Vanity, thy name is woman!"

Grass Heart laid a cold look on him as Mr. Knipp sought hastily to smother further attempts at speech from the preacher by asking her what was in the parcel that lay beside her. She had forgotten it and looked aslant at her father.

Anger darkened his face. An alert Bessie caught what passed unspoken between the two, and he tensed the muscles under the fat on his arms and legs.

"Perhaps you will open it so Mr. Knipp may see," said Good Plume, hooding his eyes and flaring his nostrils.

She unwrapped the paper, dropping it, and showed its contents, a length of red velvet, badly soiled along the edges, with golden tassels dangling from each end.

Childs let out a shriek. "A whore's sash! Evil, evil!" and smote his brow with his Bible, a solid blow that half stunned him.

Bessie sprang to his feet with a speed that astonished them all, and taking the preacher by the arm he aimed for the door, Childs still bellowing. "I seen 'em, Lord, wearin' them sashes, high-steppin' in yeller boots, whores, Lord, whores! St. Louis whores!"

The artist paused long enough to strike him forcibly in the mouth as Mr. Knipp hurried past them through the door. "Leave the horses!" he shouted. "Head for the river!" He looked back once, long enough to see the old woman on her back, her skinny legs flailing the air.

There was an empty canoe on the shore, paddles resting in its bow, and they hove the still ranting Childs aboard, Knipp pushing them into the current. Their flying paddles drenched him where he lay in the bottom of the craft, and they heard him moaning until Bessie gave him a hearty kick that stilled him.

Knipp panted. "He would have lifted our hair, by God! He knew what that idiot was hollering about all right; he's been to St. Louis twice since I come to the fort and knows what whores are and what they do. He has every right to take offense, I'd say!" Knipp ceased speaking to wield his paddle with greater speed. Bessie stepped up his pace to match and remembered the boiled dog he had escaped. His belch was harsh enough to waken a loon somewhere on the water, its crazed laughter spurring them on.

They drew the canoe up on the grassy bank on the other side of the river and left Childs in it.

"If I were you," said Bessie, which I'm not, thank God, he added silently, "I would get rid of that fool preacher, send him on his way. And give that Indian a present. They like presents. Tell him you banished Childs. He'll feel more kindly toward you for that. As for St. Louis, well, I say all men have been to a St. Louis, one way or another, in their lifetimes."

He paused to savor this thought and promised himself he would jot it down in his journal before retiring.

IN THE LODGE, Good Plume ignored Grass Heart, puffing on his stone pipe and gazing into space. She wondered what had become of Jake Moon. He was gone from where she had left him by the door, and she decided he had left when the crow-like man had started shouting so rudely. She watched Tall Hair gather herself together, muttering angrily, and stumble off into the night. It was the old woman's occasional pleasure to climb the ladder to the rooftop, where she gazed at the stars until she turned giddy and howled like a camp dog. Sometimes she came close to falling down the sides of the dome.

Grass Heart felt quite pleased with all that had occurred that evening and fell to planning what she would wear for her portrait. She thought it would be interesting to see the artist at work, for she was fond of painting too, and had recently decorated the doorposts to the lodge with colored paints, making butterflies and turtles, ruthlessly covering over the ancient stick-legged elk and square buffalo put there before her time.

Her father at last laid down his pipe and hawked, then spit neatly between his feet. "Now," he said, using the voice he employed when he tried to intimidate her, "tell me about that red sash."

She hesitated, pretending to struggle with her answer, knowing he liked to think she found it impossible to lie to him and that she came to the truth only through highly visible contest.

"Jake Moon gave it to me," she told him. "You may have seen him at

Fort Catherine, a fat white boy with a funny round hat. He's the one who stole Holy War's beaver traps and tried to trade them for a horse. He wants to marry me!" Her laughter swept around the lodge, up into the rafters, and made the mice there quiver in their nests.

Good Plume merely shrugged his shoulders. "I could use those tassels on my new leggins," he suggested.

Chagrined, she arose and stalked off to the kettle and stirred the contents with an iron spoon. Strips of bear meat rose to the surface, and she made a horrible face, saying, "Arrghhh." She refused to eat but served her father, filling his bowl mostly with the hateful gray chunks which he ate with gusto.

An argument ensued as to whether the gold tassels should go on the leggins or on the new shirt Tall Hair had just finished making him, ending with Grass Heart's assertion it would make little difference, since no other man in the village would have anything equal to them for decoration unless Jake Moon carried around more than one sash and had designs on more than one chief's daughter.

Then with triumph in her voice she asked the question he had hoped to avoid.

"Exactly what is a St. Louis whore?"

He favored her with a look she could not read, and lowered his head so the fringe of hair hid his eyes. The sash lay before him, and he took out his knife and began to cut the threads of the tassels from the velvet.

"By God, you tell me," she said.

So he did.

⌐

IN THE FORT ACROSS THE RIVER, Mr. Knipp had just poured himself a cup of brandy, put his feet up on the scarred table, and smiled to himself, remembering his first St. Louis whore. The lamp flickered with the slight wind. A shutter banged somewhere, and a fox barked in the pasture beneath the open window. "Louise," he said, and drank deeply.

Jake Moon heard the fox too from where he lay next to his hobbled mule.

He had fled the lodge at the first scream from the preacher. He was ashamed of his haste and worried what Grass Heart would think of him when she realized his absence coincided with that of the agent and his friends. Tomorrow he would go, early in the morning, and explain to her that he had not run off because he feared harm would come to him, but rather had thought it best to remove himself in deference to her father's possible anger at the three white men, to whom he was related only by the color of his skin, not by mutual cowardice.

The mule moved, her breath noisy and foul smelling, and he shifted position. Staring at the stars, he dreamed of horses.

He had always loved horses and yearned for one of those animals a man took pride in riding. Life had assigned him mules.

Once he had had a horse. It was soon after he had left home in Missouri. He had come one day to where a dainty brown mare cropped at weeds outside a fenced pasture. She wore a bridle but no saddle, and he had watched her for a long time. No one came to claim her. Before he had ridden her half a mile she threw him, and he was laid up, concealed in a damp thicket, with a sore back for two days. Since that time he had made no other effort to acquire a horse until reaching Fort Catherine.

Somewhere in his travels he had come by Posey, his mule, through a trade he chose not to think of. She had been quite agreeable to going with him. Age had been unkind to her, her hair lost to disease and hard use, clinging in strips to her hide. He felt diminished by her appearance and readily admitted that she was the ugliest animal anywhere.

On one occasion that he recalled with affection, she had carried a brace of rocking chairs nearly forty miles without complaint. A farmer's wife had given him nine dollars for them and put them in her parlor, then fed him a delicious meal of chicken and white biscuits, wringing the bird's necks with one twist of her meaty hands.

To get the mule upriver from Fort Pierre had emptied his final pocket. A river boat, outfitted with a towed barge, was going to Fort Union. The floating platform was well fenced and carried a pair of milk cows, one calf, and three horses, all tightly hobbled and tied to corner posts. After an hour of haggling, the captain of the boat at last agreed to transport Posey. Jake overlooked the man's insults. Posey proved a docile passenger, being too dispirited to cause trouble.

When they disembarked at Fort Catherine, the men of the fort heaped such ridicule on her appearance that Jake, in a fit of disgust, set out to find a proper mount. He failed in his efforts to trade the beaver traps he found in a nearby creek for one of the horses at the fort, and when a fiercely scarred Indian came forward and claimed the traps as his, it cost Jake a tin of molasses to settle the affair, although he had doubts as to the fellow's ownership.

Jake thought it unlikely he would get any sleep: Posey was uneasy, farting often, saliva dangling from her chin in long yellow ropes. He watched the sky and tried to recognize the few stars he was familiar with, but they kept changing, moving about, and he closed his eyes, falling into a stupor filled with dreams of Grass Heart and his future.

⌐

SHE WAS BUSILY LOOKING at herself in the bit of polished metal she used as a mirror. Next to her a carved deer horn held a burning pine splinter, and by its unsteady light she inspected her face, lingering over the flaw in her left eye, a tiny white oval shaped like a small seed. Her hair shone from constant greasing and she shook it approvingly, the movement setting her beads to winking.

From her painted clothes box she lifted out her finest gown, a white elk skin, bearing on its breast hundreds of elk teeth. She hung it in the doorway, the faint fragrance of rose petals and dried sage sweetening the wind.

She sensed her father watching her and knew he was scratching happily at his ears, a sign he was pleased with her, and knew he would take her to the fort tomorrow and the artist would paint her portrait after all. Grass Heart passed Tall Hair's bed as she went out the door, seeing her lying there asleep, curled up like a little rat. The old woman always accompanied her on her nightly walk to the women's trench, but this night she let her sleep.

She wanted to be alone, to taste the night on her tongue, to smell the darkness and touch the wind. As she crouched over the earthen trench she saw the Great Warrior marching across the sky, the star at the point of his lance shining the brightest of all, the moon beyond it pale and timid as though she feared his spear.

It was very late, with no one about, and a single dog howled in the village, coyotes answering from the hills. She walked past the cornfields and heard raccoons tearing at the dried stalks and the rustle of small animals in the grass. Stars wheeled above her head, and her heart suddenly lifted with an aching wonder; space and light and beauty arched over the world and the warm earth beneath her feet hummed its mysteries.

She felt she could touch the sky, could pluck from it a star, and called out to it: "Do you know me, do you see me?"

Safely in her bed she caught the light from the fast-dying fire reflected in the eyes of her father's war horse when he lifted his head over the rail, his plumed tail whispering. She heard the comforting sound of Good Plume yawning in his bed and the click-click of mice in the woodpile.

She sat up. "Father," she called, "do you know what I think? When Little Foot and those other girls at the fort do that same thing as the whores in St. Louis with Mr. Knipp's men, they get only some beads or ribbons in return. I believe that's making a very poor trade."

Good Plume said nothing, and she added, thoughtfully, "If I was ever to go to the fort to do that kind of business, I would demand a great deal of money."

Only muffled snorts of laughter came from his bed. She was taken with a fit of yawning and fell into sleep.

⌒

LAWRENCE KNIPP WAS LATE IN AWAKENING. By squinting at the slat of sun that lay over the floor of his room he guessed it was past eight o'clock, and he rose carefully from his blanket, holding his head. He thought he could feel every hair on it crackle as he moved. In the kitchen the lanky cook, his long white hair tied with a red rag at the back of his neck, brought him coffee. He ate part of a cornmeal cake put before him, hearing his teeth grinding in the empty spaces of his head. The wood fire smoked from the badly made chimney and heat filled the air. It made him nauseous. In his office he found a stool by the door, grateful for the cooler air off the river.

He looked out over the fort, wishing it was larger and the walls higher.

There were a series of small rooms that formed three sides of it, some connected by doors, the others reached only by porches set along their fronts. One room was quite large; it held the furs and trade goods. He hated to enter it, for it stunk from the buffalo hides stacked along the walls.

The rooms the men lived in were lined with rude bunks and had but single windows and doors. At the rear of the three walls, along the rooftops, a parapet ran for the guards to walk upon. Square towers stood where the corners met. The front of the fort was one long wall, broken by two gates, one narrow and seldom used, the other double-hung and constructed so that it opened inward. Outside of the narrow gate stood a small room, roofless, but with a sturdy door. It was used when Indians were troublesome and could be quickly closed in case of danger, the double gates barred from within.

The country around it was bitterly cold in winter, with heavy snows and great howling winds, and Mr. Knipp found it difficult to keep men much past autumn. Summers were hot but bearable, and they worked from first light until dark, cutting wood, putting up hay, storing it in the rude stables behind the back wall. Hunting parties went out for buffalo and elk and deer, and boats came upriver to deliver supplies and carry away the furs and hides, the heart of the business, sometimes discharging passengers, adventurers, and men seeking new horizons, discontented with the old ones.

And Indians came, from the river villages, and from the prairie dwellers: Sioux and Cheyenne, and Assiniboine from the dark, dank forests of the north, bringing their furs to trade. Few of them stayed very long, for there was bad blood between most of the tribes. But the three tribes of the rivers lived so close it made their passage easy, and they hung about, some setting up tents of animal skins and spending the summer near the fort.

Jake Moon was one of the adventurers, and so far not a successful one. He had awakened far earlier than Mr. Knipp. The wagons of the woodcutters woke him when they came out the gates, their wheels squeaking, the men grumbling, the fresh sky pink above the black trees.

Posey's gaunt sides began to heave, and he scrambled to safety before her bladder burst and she peed, a great yellow sluice, hot and steaming, next to where he had slept.

Jake wore his hat even while sleeping, and after smoothing his clothes and looking about he removed it, peering within. He carried a few flat, seed-covered cakes in his pocket and took one out, looked at it closely, and when a few crumbs appeared to move he quickly brushed them off with a finger and ate, then went to the river, knelt, and drank.

The mule did not want to go in the river when he led her to the ford, and Jake was forced to take a birch stick to her. She entered the brown summer water on trembling legs. From her high back he could see the village where it sat on a long, low hill above the shore; smoke pearled from its round-topped lodges, and the gaily colored bits of cloth tied to willow poles that rose above them fluttered in the sun.

A line of women, stooped under woven baskets, came from the gates, winding down toward the gardens in the river bottoms. To the north a wall of dark timber ran to the water's edge, protecting the village from the winds, and at the southern edge, huge rocky cliffs fell off abruptly to a spill of boulders where the river had abandoned its channel one flood-time. It was to the west of this where he and Grass Heart had walked, a few hours past, and he whistled happily, riding from shadowed to sunlit water, the sun, risen now, a perfect golden globe over the high bluffs behind the fort.

Jake reached the shore and tied Posey to a tree stub. He loitered awhile before approaching the open gates, a jaunty figure, politely smiling, the object of curious glances from the passing Indians. At last he stepped inside the palisade and stood to one side of the street, watching a group of painted warriors wearing nothing but loincloths stride by. They were tall, handsome men who talked quietly among themselves, and he eyed them with envy.

Suddenly he caught sight of Grass Heart. She wore a dress of the purest white, with animal teeth in rows across her breast, and when she looked up at his whistle of admiration she shrugged her shoulders and set them swinging. For an instant he was seized with the impression they were grinning at him. Then Grass Heart's stare rode by above them and she passed him without acknowledgment, but walked, stately and aloof, down to the shore to where her father waited, his bullboat ready for her.

Jake Moon's heart broke without a sound. His dream died, carried off on her unyielding back like a worthless bundle, his dream of her warm lodge, the long-stemmed pipe, the swift-running horse at her door, and love in a narrow bed.

He left the village and walked a long way up the river, to a grove of aspen and birch trees where a small clear stream wound over a white sand bottom. Watercress faced its edge with green, and fisher birds, hunting for minnows, cast curious, pebbled eyes on him.

"Dumb birds," he said, and sat down and cried.

Mr. Knipp was waiting for him when he at last returned to the fort.

"Come to my room," he told Jake, and in its privacy he sat him down and offered him a drink.

A melancholy Jake refused it. "I've a proposal to make you," Knipp began. Jake listened to it, fiddling with his hat.

It seemed that the present Jake had given to Good Plume's daughter had resulted in strained relations between the agent and the Indian, and to avoid any further problems Mr. Knipp felt it wise to send Jake away. He had made arrangements for him to take passage downriver that very evening, offering him a fair amount of money if he agreed.

"You can come back in the spring. It will have blown over by then." With a pause for emphasis he added shrewdly, "Got your eye on that girl of Good Plume's, I'd guess. That's another good reason it would be smart of you to disappear for a while." To himself he said, May you drown before I have to handle *that* problem too.

Jake had nothing to lose, so he agreed, a small bubble of hope rising in his breast: he would return in the spring and court Grass Heart properly. But he made Mr. Knipp promise to care for Posey while he was gone.

The agent had no idea who he meant, yet gave him his assurance, then handed Jake a sum of money quite adequate to keep him until he found work downriver.

The *Lady Elaine* was waiting below the ford. Jake boarded her, waving farewell to the strange Indians who stood on the shore. The craft had some trouble finding the main channel, turning southward finally, her whistle echoing against the cliffs and blasting the ears of the bats in their shallow caves.

Jake lost his money in a card game the first night on the river.

⌐

GOOD PLUME SAT in the sunshine in front of his lodge, brooding on Grass Heart's behavior of the previous night, subtly aware he had little control over her any longer, and fearing the time when some unscrupulous white man would beguile her into a less-than-honorable situation. The idea angered him, and he stuck his forefinger in his mouth and bit it, hard.

Nearby children shouted and he heard a strange rumbling, then saw a cart, drawn by an ox, coming up the street. It stopped before his lodge. Mr. Knipp sat on its box beside one of his men from the fort. Good Plume knew at a glance that this was to be a formal visit. The agent wore his embroidered waistcoat, a piece of clothing reserved for serious occasions.

Two resplendent peacocks glittered from the waistcoat, their beaks facing, their many-colored tails disappearing in his armpits. He raised his right arm to remove his hat, and their golden eyes blinked in wicked repetition. "Chief," he said.

A grave-faced Good Plume nodded to him, and the two men got down and went to the rear of the cart. From it they lifted a door, hewn of oak, with metal hinges and a black iron latch and bolt.

Grass Heart had heard the noise and now stood by her father. Her face as quiet as his, she watched the agent brush his hands anxiously across the splendid peacocks and slap them smartly to remove whatever dust they may have collected.

"Please accept this small gift as a symbol of my good will toward your lodge, and also my apology for last night's unfortunate incident," he said.

"This door will keep out the winter's snow, and those you don't want in your home," he added, and winked significantly at the girl.

Good Plume allowed a small smile to lift a corner of his mouth, and Mr. Knipp settled down on his heels beside him. They watched Frankie Paradise while he measured the doorposts and the door itself for a proper fit. As he hammered away he covertly listened to the conversation between the men.

Suddenly an old woman, her head shaven and one cheek painted a bright blue, surged out the doorway, frightening him. She ran, leaping from side to side, off down the street, and Frankie saw to his astonishment that her bare feet were painted blue also.

He did not like the Mandan Indians, and, if asked, readily admitted he hated all Indians. And here he was, nailing this door to the front of one of their lodges, a door that had sat in a storeroom at the fort for years, ever since it had been rescued from the Little Fort of Lewis and Clark and brought upriver before the Indians tore down the buildings for firewood. He snarled at a reluctant nail, reminding himself it was none of his business what Mr. Knipp gave away.

The sun was bearing off the afternoon when the cart creaked off toward the river. Grass Heart swung the door back and forth, locking and unlocking the inside bolt, until she tired of it.

"I believe I was too friendly to him," her father said when she brought him the pipe he asked for.

"Where did that old piss-pot woman go?" demanded Grass Heart. "I wish you would tell her—"

"Stop!" he shouted. "Those words! Where do you get them?" he asked in despair. "Such bad language!"

She opened her eyes very wide. "From those white men, those friends of yours and the others who visit here."

"Don't use them. Please."

She made an ugly face where he could not see her. "That Tall Hair is to fetch water and runs off. She gets lazier every day. I give her bloody hell and it changes nothing. You speak to her."

Next she'll ask me to beat the old fool, he told himself. And I order her not to swear and she pays no mind. If only her mother was here, she would know how to teach her. It's too late for me to change her ways.

He had done the best he could. It was painful to admit it had not been good enough, and he turned to thinking of more easily resolved matters, musing on his association with the agent, and fretting whether he should have accepted the door from him or not.

Mr. Knipp was congratulating himself on his handling of a potentially damaging situation, so far as his business went, and offered a green cigar to Paradise, even setting a match to it for him, as the assistant struggled with the oxen reins. They jolted over the rocks, down to the ford. Paradise, encouraged by the gesture of familiarity the cigar represented, felt bold enough to ask, "Why did you give that door away to them Indians?"

"To mend relations," Knipp answered, puffing rapidly at his cigar.

"But they ain't no kin to you," Paradise scowled, and the agent began to howl with laughter, nearly falling from the cart, losing his cigar to the river.

Tall Hair came back finally, slinking into the lodge. Grass Heart sent her for water, and when she returned with the full buffalo bladders hanging from a green branch across her thin shoulders the door would not yield to her push. She kicked at it, stubbing her toes, till Grass Heart tired of her screeching and unlocked it.

The old woman brought out her ax from beneath her bed and threatened to chop down the door, until Good Plume pushed her outside and took away her weapon. Tall Hair walked, cursing, back to the creek and sat on the sandy bank under a drooping willow tree. Soon a group of village women appeared, carrying clay pots and clanking shiny tin pails, and with sidelong disapproval they passed their eyes over her blue cheek and shorn hair. One, more curious than the rest, asked about the door, and Tall Hair sniffed and picked at her nose. Then the woman asked what the white men had been doing at Good Plume's lodge the past night.

"They left their horses," another said, "can you believe that! Left their horses and stole Red Thunder's good canoe."

"And those two loafers they sent to get the horses gave Red Thunder two measures of gunpowder! He is hoping they will steal it again, and leaves it unprotected on the bank for anybody to take."

They looked at one another and giggled.

Tall Hair could stand it no longer. "They hit me," she wailed, and pointed to places on her legs and arms where she thought it possible she was bruised. "I had to run away and hide on the roof!" In her excitement spit flew from her mouth. "And Good Plume and that girl, they quarreled. It was terrible. *She is a witch.*"

The women strained to hear. "I saw her," Tall Hair whispered, and their heads bent lower and encircled her. "I saw her throw mud on Okeedah, the Evil One! She thinks nobody saw her, but I did, I spied on her, and she did it." The lie became a certainty with her words, and she hid her head in her skirt.

Then there was a low hissing from the women, like a bag full of angry snakes, and they went "Loo, loo, loo," and made signs against bad luck with their fingers.

They carried off their pails and pots, hurriedly, leaving Tall Hair under the tree, her bare scalp still in her skirt until she raised it, vaguely surprised to find herself alone, and went back to picking her nose.

⤸

SUMMER LOST HER SEASON; the first frost had come and gone, and a haze lay over the land, warm and blue, and the vines turned scarlet and clung more closely to the trees along the river, its water reflecting the pure deep blue of the autumn sky.

The ghost of winter lit his fires in the northern sky, and the people watched them at night, then hurried to count their fur robes and make secure the pits of grain and seeds inside the lodges.

Prairie fires, set by the hunters, raged on the cured grasses, and the thunder of running buffalo mingled with the smoke. The women gathered the ripe berries from the bushes along the river bottoms; the harvest was done, and the last of the fruit filled their baskets and their mouths. Huge bears fed on the berries too, ignoring the women, so that a mutual feast took place, a tenuous peace governing all.

Good Plume spent the days lying on the roof of the lodge, smoking, watching, and reflecting on his life.

Most of his thoughts concerned Grass Heart.

Her mother had died soon after her birth, from the bite of a rabid wolf. They had been returning from a visit to her grandmother, a Cheyenne, whose band was summering on the Bad River. The wolf had wandered into their camp at daylight, and she had just finished nursing Grass Heart and went out to care for their horses when the animal appeared.

Good Plume heard her shrieks and ran from the pond where he had been washing himself to find her on her knees, facing the wolf. He killed it with one blow of his ax.

He had been too late. She died in agony, leaving him bereft of all reason, and it was only his daughter's presence in his life that prevented him from taking his.

Now, in the autumn, both of the season and of his years, he counted on his fingers the summers that had passed, and was shocked to find them fourteen.

He had come to love his daughter blindly, the pride he had in her clouding his eyes. He spoiled her, indulged her, refused to find any faults in her.

When she had fallen in love with Bloody Dog (whom Good Plume could never reconcile with Sweet Flag), his despair had been knotted with sympathy. For some months now, he reflected, she had been going off to the women's lodge beyond the cornfields to return a few days later with a smug look to her. And when Mr. Bessie painted her, she had dressed, with new modesty, out of Good Plume's sight, but he had been conscious nevertheless of the knobby breasts under the elk teeth.

He had always been terrified he would die before she had someone who loved her as well as he and would care for her. Faced with her inevitable marriage, he decided to take charge of what could not be avoided, and spoke to her.

"It is time you took a husband," he said, and she took note of the melancholy in his voice and shook her head in negation. "We must look to your future. I will not always be here to care for you; you need a young man to do that."

Grass Heart said, "I don't want to marry," but in secret she wondered what it would be like. Many of her friends were wed, and they whispered and teased one another before her. "You act different," she complained. Then they became dignified and superior, and their bellies bulged with babies, and her indignation decreased as their stomachs enlarged, proportionately.

Young warriors soon began to come to her lodge at dusk, the first tentative peeping of the love flutes chilling Good Plume's blood. At first Grass Heart loitered behind the door, pretending a meekness he knew her incapable of, but soon had to abandon it, for he would go out and ask questions of them, very improperly, disconcerting them so they faded into the darkness, the flutes silent. She scolded him, saying, "You frighten them away, you drive them off and I don't know who they are. You insist I take a husband, then make sure I don't."

"Don't concern yourself," he told her. "I know what I am doing." He had persuaded himself he was protecting her from making a wrong choice; he would help her in her decision, while he prevented her from making one at all.

"It's not you they are courting. Nobody wants to marry you."

"I can take a wife if I wanted to. Many a time I've thought of it." He laughed lightly.

"Who would have you, you ugly old man." She was glaring fiercely at him, the flaw in her eye white as stone.

He knew full well how jealous she was at the idea of his marrying again, and he gave her a smile that was entirely false. "I have any number of women just waiting," he said.

But she had recognized the smile for what it was and turned her back on him. "Go on," she said. "Get a new wife. By the time you find one, by God, I'll be old and ugly." He didn't reply, and she knew she had beat him again.

Tall Hair was listening from her place by the door and snickered loudly, rapping her fists against the post. Perhaps they will hit one another, she thought in glee and waited for the first blow, but Grass Heart took a fish line and a handful of bone hooks from a pouch and stalked from the lodge.

"She needs a husband," Tall Hair told Good Plume. "One that will hit her every day."

"Leave!" he shouted, shaking a fist at her. "Go away, out of my lodge!"

There was nowhere to go but to the creek, and she waited for the women to come for water. She would tell them about the fight. It had been a long time since they had thrown rocks at her.

Among Grass Heart's suitors was one who would have fitted the old woman's requirement and who came the closest to marrying the girl, except that he ran into a piece of good luck that turned out to be bad luck and led to his losing her.

He was a young warrior called True Bear, a fine-looking youth who came from a family of notable fighters. His father and grandfather, not content with their accumulated honors, continued their reckless exploits, and as a consequence True Bear was denied a rightful place among those who did battle with the enemy. It ate at him and honed his already keen temper, and he fought with his brothers and sisters over trifles.

When he had reached manhood, he had taken the Thunderbird for his spirit teacher, believing it would elevate his standing in his family and in the village. It changed nothing. The rivalry, especially in the lodge, increased, so True Bear in desperation set out to marry and have his own lodge, where peace and respect were his unconditionally.

Storms were frequent that late summer, and his vow to the Thunderbird was kept faithfully, so that he often slept on the riverbank beneath the lightning and the rolling thunder of the storms. One night as he lay there waiting for a voice from his spirit teacher, his mind was occupied with thoughts of Grass Heart, whom he had determined to marry. The spirit's arrows of lightning crashed around him and he felt his scalp prickle ominously. He was not frightened, until thunder shook the ground and the earth growled beneath him and he was thrust from his blanket by its monstrous ripple. He looked into the dark throat of the sky and waited.

Suddenly he heard faint shouting coming from the river, and but for the direction of the wind he would have missed it. A shaft of yellow light showed a boat, looming above a sandbar.

After the storm diminished, he swam out to the wreckage, all thoughts of duty and love washed away. Whoever had been aboard the small boat was gone, and in the growing light of dawn he searched it, finding nothing of value. True Bear felt cheated. He stood on the sandbar and shook his hatchet in anger.

A movement in the corner of his eye set him as still as a rock. Then he turned his head very slowly. A man stood nearby, peering sideways at him, and True Bear raised his hatchet, set his feet in the firm sand, and with open mouth bellowed a challenge to fight. The other did the same, soundlessly, and he put out his hand in wonderment and touched the glass. It was a mirror, full length and whole, set in a wooden frame and resting in the sand. True Bear stooped and smiled into its surface.

It changed his entire life.

Someone heard at last his yells and came in a bullboat and freighted his prize home. The people were wary of the mirror when they first saw it, and eyed it respectfully. True Bear gained stature from its ownership. He spent hours before it. He began to invent new hairstyles, each more elaborate than the one before, fashioned with mud and clay into tall, intricate coils, top-heavy with ornaments. One day his eldest sister struck his youngest sister in the face while fighting over who should use the mirror first. The youngest lost her eye. It fell out of its socket into the dirt of the floor, and a rat snatched it up and ran off with it.

Wounded though she was, the sister saw well enough to hack the fateful mirror into small pieces with True Bear's hatchet. Then she went out into the woods and hanged herself.

True Bear underwent a shunning so severe that he left the village and was absent for a long while, and on his return married The Mink, a shrew who was much older than he. She never bathed and smelled like a dung heap. An outcast from his family, he lived a wretched life.

Good Plume had thought highly of True Bear, but after his decline into a vain, self-centered dandy, he seemed to lose interest in Grass Heart's string of suitors, and she was quite satisfied to wait for another summer, and better choices.

⤔

THE WEATHER-KEEPER CONSULTED the ancient gray-feathered owl that lived in his lodge, tied by a foot to a high rafter. The bird foretold a long, severe winter, with heavy snows and great winds. After giving the owl a live mouse and tying him up again, he went out with his drum, a cottonwood hoop with deerskin stretched over it, and called out his predictions, going up and down each street.

Good Plume cast his own weather by going out on the prairie and measuring the height of certain plants and observing the color and thickness of the coats of various animals. He admitted only to himself the reason for doing so: he detested moving to the winter village, miles downstream. The quarters there were cramped and dull, the lodges small and stuffy, and too many quarrels and feuds developed from the overcrowding.

That year he found no signs indicating the Weather-Keeper was right, so while the people who were going readied themselves for travel, he was helping Tall Hair count the robes and supplies of meat and dried food. He found them more than adequate. She had worked very hard, harder than usual, and he spoke kindly to her about it, exciting her so that she ran from the lodge with her soiled skirt over her face and fell over the rack near the door.

There were plenty of others in the village who preferred to remain behind also, and they gathered on the prescribed day to watch those who were going begin their journey downstream. The old men led first, their horses prancing, their women and the children walking and leading pack animals or ponies who dragged travois. Camp dogs barked and fought as the older children drove them forward, some of the animals loaded with utensils and clothing rattling along behind. On the upper reaches of the prairie the young men herded the huge bands of horses, their hooves sending clouds of dust from the dry powdery soil far into the bright sky. The shouts and yells and cries and chatter could be heard long after their makers passed from sight, the noise suspended in the bright chill air, fading into ghostly sounds, until there was nothing but the sigh of the wind and the steady whisper of the river.

HUNDREDS OF MILES DOWN THAT SAME river Jake Moon's luck had turned sour again. He had burned down his place of employment.

It began when the captain of the *Lady Elaine* refused him further passage and sent him ashore at Fort Pierre.

He had no money, no prospects, and no one to welcome him when he stepped on land. Reminding himself he was no stranger to hard times, he brushed off his clothing, settled his hat on his round head, and looked about for some means to support himself.

The fort was somewhat changed from his earlier visit: more of the tall, closed-faced Sioux stood against the wall of the sutler's store, and it seemed there were half-breed children everywhere he looked. The fur trappers, dark as Indians, wearing gaudy ribboned caps and short capes of striped blanket cloth dazzled Jake, and he yearned to be of their company, rather than that of common fellows like himself, with dirty cloth coats and worn boots.

After some days of going hungry, he at last found work in a mule yard, feeding the beasts and mucking up after them, his pay minimal. He was allowed to sleep in the shed where hay was stored, and considered himself fortunate, for it was warm and dry, and the weather leaning toward winter.

Sometimes the lack of a solid future weighed him down, and he resorted to drink, laying about the following day, his head reeling from cheap liquor. He shied pebbles at the mules as they milled around, restless from the stink of the whisky that enwrapped him. They identified the smell with clubs and whips, and honked and squealed till Jake retreated to the darkest corner of the shed and fell asleep.

One night he met a small, dull-witted man who taught him to smoke cigars. He became attached to the habit and smoked around the yard, until he accidentally dropped a live spark in a bale of hay and set it afire. It spooked the mules. They surged through a weakened section of fencing he had intended to fix but had neglected, and went raging through the settlement, damaging porches and boardwalks, late gardens and lines of freshly washed clothing. Cast out, he wandered the settlement.

A Mrs. Rosen, attracted by his forlorn appearance, called out to him one day as he was passing and placed a plate of food in his hands. "Eat!" she commanded.

She ran a cook shack where hungry trappers and boatmen came to stand along the raw pine shelves she had nailed to the wall and eat the simple foods she sold. She was a sturdy woman, short in stature, and wore men's trousers and men's boots, in which she stumped back and forth between the stove and the shelves. Her command of vulgar oaths was formidable; she reserved them for the balky stove and ungentlemanly customers and was known to belong to an obscure religion, often talking in tongues while stirring a kettle of beans or frying elk steaks. She fed Jake Moon because he reminded her of a saint, his clear blue eyes and crown of thorny spiked hair plucking at her pious heart.

It was she who suggested he move in with Willow Woman, a half-breed with two small sons of unknown ancestry, who sometimes cleaned for Mrs. Rosen in return for leftovers, and who he met that evening, while eating.

So low had Jake fallen that he assented to care for Willow Woman's children while she tended her business, a casual whoring among the boatmen, the woodcutters, and others of simple, inexpensive tastes.

All she asked of Jake was to watch over her boys; she was an excellent mother and loved them dearly.

He found time to go hunting, hoping to put food on the table in exchange for his shelter, walking the browned, ice-crusted grass of the sloughs along the lowlands, where grouse and prairie chickens strutted in the late afternoon sun. He found he was a poor shot but enjoyed the solitary walks, the pure cold air tingling his cheeks and untangling his thoughts. His heart was lighter and his troubles less when he returned to the shack, never suspecting the reason he missed the birds he aimed at lay in the old gun he carried, one Willow Woman had traded a robe for and whose barrel was rusted out.

"It don't matter none," she told him when he apologized for his empty hands. "I kin git one o' my uncles to give me part of a antelope."

But Jake Moon felt useless and sat on his broken chair, staring out a broken window. He wondered what he could do to make life easier for Willow Woman and her boys, who amused themselves the greater share of the time, seldom speaking to him.

He sought to give more purpose to their lives by teaching them to read and write. They told him gently, "It won't do us no good. Us'ns is too dumb." It puzzled him where they had learned to speak in those words. It was as though they came straight out of the Arkansas backwoods. It remained a mystery, for he never got up the nerve to ask.

The shack they occupied was but two rooms, with cracks in the walls and a roof that let in the rain and wind. There was but one window that wasn't boarded over, and it held oiled paper that was cracked and leaked.

He promised himself he would make it more livable. An empty house nearby furnished boards and nails and shingles. By the time the first snow fell, Jake had repaired the roof and walls and had sealed the windows tight. In a summer kitchen used infrequently by the sutler's Indian wife (who could not reconcile herself to cooking under a roof), he found a fine stove and brought it home, chimney pipe and all, one black night, in a wheelbarrow he found. He installed it in the room where they all slept and split wood for it that he took from a pile stacked behind a neighbor's shed, figuring it would not be missed if he limited his borrowing to reasonable amounts.

Willow Woman was delighted with the new accommodations and put off her plans to spend the winter with relatives in their camp far off in the Black Hills. The house was snug and warm, her children happy and content. The winter would pass quickly this year, she thought with pleasure.

She looked at Jake sitting in a rocking chair that she assumed someone had thrown away and he mended. He held a sad-iron, her sons cracking acorns on it. The stove burbled and glowed, and she yawned, her strong white teeth wide apart.

"There's nothin' nicer thin a good fire, less'n it's a little lovin'," she said. She winked at Jake, her eye opening and closing like a round shutter. He blushed.

"I'm engaged to be married," he said hastily, startling himself with such a lie.

"Some gel is lucky to git sech a gin'rous feller," Willow Woman told him.

Gesturing around the shabby room, he said, "Now you can live like a queen!"

She smiled a small, plump-cheeked smile and went to her bed, lay down, and promptly fell asleep.

"Doesn't your mama look sweet lying there?" Jake asked Homer, the eldest of the two, who looked at his mother, then said, "Thet she do."

Later, while rocking alone by the fire, Jake heard the wind calling from the spaces of the long night, and thought of Grass Heart, hoping she thought of him sometimes too, and tried to recall her face. Only pieces of it came to him: the curve of her jaw, the planes of a cheekbone, the angle of an eyelid.

They were enough to swell his heart with longing, and he groaned, while Willow Woman dreamt of a lost lover, and bedbugs, awakened from their winter stupor by the heat from the stove, feasted steadily on the tender flesh of Homer and his brother.

$\backsim$

FAR UP THE HALF-FROZEN RIVER, Grass Heart and her father enjoyed mild weather. They visited with others in the village, played stone games, and watched a magician remove live birds and other strange objects from his stomach, drawing them from his mouth amid clouds of smoke. As always there was much gambling—on horse races when the ground was dry and the weather warm, and on such minor matters as to whether a wolf or coyote would howl first in the evening, or if one man's bullboat was swifter than another's.

Grass Heart learned to quill, under the tutelage of a woman who lived in the lodge next to hers, but her long, irregular stitches never pleased her teacher, and they both lost interest in her pursuit. She never made anything worthwhile that winter.

Toward the end, a blizzard struck, coming out of the gray northwest, a warm rain preceding it. The village was buried under the snow, the fort isolated. Activity out of doors ceased.

Mr. Knipp read and reread the few books the men owned, turning finally to the Bible the cook offered him. He found it so depressing he hastily returned it and went to drinking, sleeping long hours.

His men lay about, grumbling and plotting, springing into unexplainable, desperate fights.

Frankie Paradise seemed to be content, though. He was involved in a plan which he had drawn up on paper that would divert the river downstream near the ford. He would import a gristmill and set it up there, then buy corn from the Indians' gardens the following summer and make his own liquor from it to sell at huge profits. When he approached Mr. Knipp with his finished plans, the agent, his blood sluggish with rum, grunted meanly and sent him away.

Grass Heart's pony, a new black-and-white-spotted animal she had won from her father, was missing the day after the snow fell. She complained bitterly. Her father had been at fault for not shutting the mare in the lodge along with his, but left tied to the rack by the door.

"She has only run off with the wind," he assured her. "She will come back when she can."

"Somebody stole her," insisted Grass Heart. "I'd like to catch the thief, I'd cut off his bloody balls!"

He told her to watch her tongue, that she spoke words that even the most ignorant, ill-mannered white man would not use around him, and they had a staring match that ended when she laid aside the spoon and dish she had been eating from and went to sit on the other side of the fire.

She coughed noisily, and clutched at her throat as though in pain. "I believe I am getting sick," she whimpered. She knew how it terrified him if she showed any indication of sickness, and she coughed again.

He listened, suspecting her of shamming, and the coughs continued, rising in intensity. He stood up and called to Tall Hair.

"Bring me my robe and boots," he ordered. The old woman stumbled about, hunting up his winter clothing, whining about her aching bones, until Grass Heart shouted at her.

She had regretted her words and her silly coughing immediately after her father had spoken to the slave, and shame made her hiccup, little sounds she muffled in her hands.

Good Plume had dressed and slipped a rope bridle over his black horse, leading it from the pen by the door, and did not hear her sudden call to him, asking him to wait, not to go. He led the animal out the door, the wind slipping past him and throwing a drift of white into the lodge. It made the smoke swirl yellow and the fire jump high.

Tall Hair crouched over it, started up, her face knuckled in thought. She had remembered something important but did not speak. Instead, she turned her nose back to the fire, mumbling in distress.

All through the afternoon Grass Heart took quick peeks out the door, cracking it for one eye. The whirling snow blinded her; the wind carried the moan of the frozen trees along the river. She stamped about the lodge, overturning whatever lay in her path in her frustration. Then panic settled like a fever in her when Good Plume did not return, and it set her to crying. Tall Hair woke long enough to ask her what was wrong.

"He is never coming back! I drove him off!" she wept.

"She ran off," Tall Hair replied.

"My father, you fool, not my pony!" and Grass Heart aimed a blow at the old woman that glanced off her cheek but made her howl anyway.

Suddenly she stopped; her cloudy black eyes rolled back in their wrinkled sockets and she went in haste to her bed box, where she lay down and covered her face with her robe. In its warm, sour-smelling depths she saw, quite plainly, the foot covers that belonged to the tall horse Good Plume rode. Stained with manure and urine, they rested in the darkest corner of the stall where she had thrown them. She thought: He will slip on the ice. She tried to sleep, her ears muffled against the girl's cries.

It grew cold in the lodge, and Grass Heart wiped her face on her sleeve, rose, and threw dry wood on the fire. She put on her hooded blanket coat and heavy fur boots and went out the door, pulling it shut behind her. The frozen wind stole her breath and wove ice crystals on the fur about her face. She ran when the wind lessened and rested when it lifted the snow, and at last she found the fence of rough wood and followed it to the river gate, open in winter.

The shrill squeals of the black horse led her at last to Good Plume. The animal lay on its side on the ice, a broken foreleg like a lifted arm beckoning to her.

Her father was on his back next to it, and she knelt down, lifted his hood, and looked into his face. He smiled.

"You will have to kill him," he said.

"No," she said, giving him the corners of her eyes, the smoke of her breath escaping on the wind.

"Yes," he said, and her stomach hollowed beneath her ribs, and her heart fell down into it.

Good Plume reached to his belt and lifted up the sharp-bladed ax. She took it dumbly into her mittened hand. The palm was wet from snow, and the ax handle slid when she struck at the horse with it. The blade grazed the bony forehead, a trickle of blood rising from the gash.

"Not there," Good Plume said. "Strike him in the neck, cut as deeply as you can."

His voice steadied her and she struck where he pointed, again and again, the scarlet liquid, hot and steaming, spurting upward, staining her coat, her sleeves, a pool slowly spreading about her boots. The smell filled her mouth and she licked her lips, seeing the blade bite into the ragged red hole.

With a final heave, the horse shuddered once more and lay still, his eyes the color of old ice, his tongue lolling in the snow.

She dropped the ax, turned away and vomited, then sat, quivering, for a long time in the snow, dimly aware of the blood that saturated it.

"You are not very good at killing," said Good Plume after a while.

"I learned, though," she said, her face telling him nothing.

"Hand me the ax," he asked her with a wry grin. "My leg is broken also."

There were hollow spaces in her look that had never been there before as she handed it to him. "Let us go home," she said and went to where her pony stood, fastening a long rope from its neck to her father's belt. The animal trembled and fought her when it smelled the blood she carried, and with brutal jerks she brought it to where her father lay after tying shut her nose with rawhide. She lifted Good Plume and helped him over the pony's back, his feet furrowing the whiteness with crooked rows as they headed back.

Darkness fell before they reached the gate. In exhaustion she forced the pony through the deep streets to their lodge. Tall Hair brewed a drink of herbs that put him to sleep, while Grass Heart cut the wet clothing from him, handling the bent leg with care. The exposed knee showed no bones penetrating the skin, but the shape of it was wrong, and she called the old woman to come with a pine knot and hold its light so she could see.

Grass Heart saw the knee curved outward; it felt soft and wobbled beneath her gentle probing. She covered his frostbitten nose and cheeks with bear grease, and when he seemed to be resting comfortably she took off her own outer clothing and washed the blood spots from her face and hands.

All night she sat next to where he slept, and when morning came and she looked outside, the wind had disappeared with the darkness. The sky was clear, blue-streaked with the first sun rays glittering across it as it cleared the black cliffs beyond the fort. In the valley, the river wound its shadow between the black trees draped with snow.

The pony stood where she had been tied, and Grass Heart regarded her thoughtfully before going to the woodpile where she chose a stout club. She beat the animal with measured strokes until it broke loose and ran, snorting and biting at its haunches, out the rear gate toward the prairie. She watched her out of sight, then sank down into the snow and raised her eyes to the wavering threads of geese and cranes, rowing with their wings the river of the sky, northwards to spring.

Something had happened to her, she knew. Something so important she had no name for it, a thing so dreadful and terrifying that she pushed it from her mind. But it had changed her, making her more, or less, she did not know, and she shivered as though a ghost had touched her arm.

⌒

IT WAS TALL HAIR, IN THE END, who determined Grass Heart's immediate future. The old slave had spent too many winters over smoky fires, and her eyesight grew a gray skin, so that she did not realize the river ice was rotten and ventured out on it, talking to herself and waving her arms heedlessly. The river gave an ominous groan and swallowed her up.

She was not missed until the evening meal. Grass Heart warmed the cold stew, burning the bottom of the kettle. After her father finished eating, she carried the blackened pot to the rear fence and threw it in the dump ground. A neighbor finally reported that Tall Hair had fallen through the ice, and Grass Heart, in a rare display of conscience, told her father she was sorry the old slave was gone and wished she had treated her better.

But suddenly burdened with tasks she was unfit for, Grass Heart applied herself to solving the problems that faced her. She knew nothing of caring for a lodge, and her father, because of his leg, could no longer hunt for meat for them.

The people had come back from the winter village, and coolly she appraised the young men among them, settling on one with four older sisters, two who were widows with little chance of remarrying.

Star Blanket was a proven hunter, and that weighed heavily in his favor. Otherwise, there was nothing remarkable about him. Good Plume thought him one of those youths whose outlines are dim and unstable, and one was never sure what their futures might be, since they took so long to develop one.

The four sisters were of little account, too, the widows and the unmarried ones. They were homely and considered dull-witted. The youngest wore a growth on her cheek like moss on a dead tree, and Good Plume's only stipulation to the marriage was that she be excluded from his lodge.

It surprised Star Blanket how quickly it all happened. He had no sooner gotten down from his horse than Grass Heart strolled by and spoke to him, smiling sweetly and fluttering her lashes. She asked him how it had been in the winter village.

"Like always," he said, too astonished to add anything more. Her casual chatter bewildered him, and when she asked him if he would like to call on her that evening, he managed only to say "Yes."

She went home, rather pleased it took so little to charm him, and before he fully apprehended what was happening, they were married.

He hadn't even had time to unwrap and hang up his shield, and he was a husband! he told Magpie, the widowed sister, and he urged her to pack her belongings and come live with him in his wife's lodge. She complied without a murmur.

"She is a chief's daughter and not accustomed to cooking and such things," Star Blanket said. He thought perhaps he could capture some woman from another tribe sometime that summer on a raid, although he was not sure how one went about it. Then Magpie could take her ease, too.

On the fifth night, after whispered urgings by his sister, Star Blanket made his way in the darkness to avail himself of a husband's privilege.

After making certain Good Plume slept, he went to his bride's bed. He climbed atop her, breathless, and found her wrapped within her sleeping robe. She woke and made an impatient noise and he entered her. Immediately he felt a slight tickle and then a limpness overcame his member. Grass Heart waited but nothing happened. She gave him a solid shove to the floor, where his foot caught a box of iron arrowheads, upsetting them. He thought he would faint.

Safe in his own bed he vowed he would never try that again: the danger was too great and the reward too small.

Grass Heart saw the moon cross the roof's smoke hole. So that's what it is like, she thought in disgust, and pursed her lips and made a rude noise. A muffled giggle came from Magpie's bed.

"Shut up," she said crossly. "One fool a night is all I can stand."

⤚

JAKE MOON WATCHED WILLOW WOMAN put on the old bearskin coat she wore to work when the nights were cold. It was thickly furred, indeterminate in color, and harbored generations of lively fleas that floated off in the bitter wind like sugar crystals.

Sometimes he went with her as far as Mrs. Rosen's, where he sat by the cookstove and drank bitter coffee she gave him in a dainty, flowered cup she kept in a drawer with a loaded pistol, several silver spoons, and a piece of embroidered muslin she pinned over her hair when entertaining him.

One morning he awoke to find the air had turned soft, a fresh wind blowing it from the south. Birds sang and leaves appeared, drawn by a sun bright as a gold coin against the blue sky, and winter was gone for another year.

Jake helped Willow Woman drag out all their bedclothes into the yard, where they draped them from thickets and branches in the sunshine. The boys ran about grinning, and they all took turns picking the lice from one another's hair. With water fetched from the melted river and heated on the stove, they bathed in turn, Jake first.

He sat in fresh clothing on the narrow stoop and lazily thought of Grass Heart, and Posey, the only thing he owned of value. He remembered her as a more agreeable and sturdy beast than she was in the flesh, even as a friend, one who would never let him down, like some he could name, then scratched at his head trying to think of anyone he knew who had deceived him recently. He was relieved when none came to mind.

When the boats came upriver, he had no money for passage on one, and it was summer before he managed it, and then only through the generosity of Mrs. Rosen.

She set a rawhide pouch before him, next to his coffee cup one evening. "Willow Woman told me you had important business at Fort Catherine." She adjusted her muslin cap, her eyes lowered. Jake noticed a raw burn on her hand, and she hastily hid it in her lap. "I took up a collection. 'Tis there."

He hefted the pouch and it clinked merrily. "I can't take your money, it wouldn't be fair."

"'Tisn't to take, 'tis a loan."

"I can't pay you back," he said to the pouch, and laid it back on the scarred table. "The only thing I have is a mule."

"Argghhh," she said, "I don't want no mule."

"Well, that's all I have."

"Willow Woman says you are to marry up there. The daughter of a chief. That means a dowry. Write me out on a piece of paper and put your name to it. Furs," she ordered, and sucked at her coffee.

She peeped at him over the rim of her cup, seeing him deliberate. Jesus must have looked like that in the temple. A saintly lad, she was thinking.

Jake counted the money. It was more than enough for his fare. He could buy new clothes too.

"All right," he said.

She had a bit of paper and a pencil ready and bent her neck to watch him as he printed the words out, laboring over them. He handed the scrap to her and laid the pencil next to his cup.

After he was gone, she rinsed out the cups and sat in the lamplight, studying what he had written. Then she began to sing, a melancholy hymn about death and retribution and punishment, in a nasal voice that carried strong and clear out into the warm night.

Before she lay down on her single cot she put the piece of paper in the drawer with her other heirlooms. It rested atop a stack of similar notes.

"'Tis another," she said, and shut the drawer. "An innocent babe."

It was mid-July before Jake went aboard the *St. Peter*, dressed in a new jacket with grosgrain trim, wearing a hat, unstained and bearing goose feathers in its band. He sauntered to the bow and waved good-bye to Willow Woman and her sons, until the boat steamed out of sight.

There were times to come when he would recall her with affection, believing the world would have been better with more of her kind in it.

THE RIVER VILLAGES WAITED FOR THE BUFFALO to move to their hunting grounds, but only scattered bands were found. The Sioux, always a threat to the people, ranged far to the west, running the herds to keep them from the river, and White Cow, the head chief of the Mandan, called the council members to their lodge to discuss a solution, deciding with little disagreement it had become necessary to hold the ceremony known as Dancing the Buffalo to persuade the herds to come to them.

The young eligible warriors were brought into the lodge where White Cow stood, surrounded by the elders. He held a woven basket, covered with weasel skins. The head of a great prairie wolf rested over them, the jaws open. The youths were instructed on how to reach between them into the basket, to draw out a stone and hold it up for all to see. All were white but one. It was black, and when Star Blanket stuck a nervous hand within the pointed teeth, he brought it out.

He did not fully understand the meaning of it until White Cow embraced him and spoke of the honor his selection bestowed on him and clapped Star Blanket on his narrow, bony back. It was the first time the young man had seen the metal tooth the old chief wore in the front of his mouth, so was not aware of the jealous looks and whispered complaints of his fellow warriors.

It came to him that now he would be accorded the respect he deserved from Grass Heart and Good Plume, but to his dismay he was sworn to secrecy. He could not reveal any part of his coming role to anyone, leaving him no better off than before.

Star Blanket retreated to the prairie during the first three days of the ceremony, where he fasted and prayed. On the fourth day he became the Buffalo Spirit.

He stood on the hill west of the village, dressed in his costume, trembling with excitement. Bare but for a loincloth, his head was encased in the massive head of a bull buffalo, held upright by a wooden frame beneath it. The eye holes were slits through which he peered, his vision limited by their small size. A magnificent beard hung below the chin and tickled his hairless chest. Huge pointed horns shone in the bright sun. He had polished them with sand and spit and soft deerskin. A tail dangled from his buttocks and between his legs rode a long wooden rod, tipped with a red painted knob. On his feet were false hooves.

Someone from the people gathered on the dancing ground spied him, and a roar rose from the crowd. He began to run down the slope.

Down there waited the Buffalo Dancers, wearing the capes and heads of cows, pawing at the ground, snorting, simulating the full heat of the mating season.

The knob on his wooden rod bounced over the rocks and he guided it carefully with both hands around the shaft. Sweat ran into his eyes; the head was hot and close, and he could scarcely breathe, but he trotted on, panting.

When he reached the circle he stamped his hooves and snorted, ineffectually, since his nose was stopped up with dirt. He charged wildly into the cow buffalo and lunged at their backsides with his rod. One by one they paused long enough to bend over, and, sticking the rod through their legs, he pretended to copulate with them, making the crowd cheer wildly. His legs weakened and his neck ached with the weight of the head, but he continued until all were serviced.

The cows showed fatigue and contentment and drooped their heads, staggering away. He turned to the women, who shoved and pushed to get near him, and teased them with swift rushes, waving his rod. They shrieked and ran away, and then stones and sticks hit him, and welts grew, and he was blinded by the dirt thrown at his mask. Suddenly his sight was completely blocked, and he gave a feeble roar and stood still, weaving with exhaustion. A brutal jerk made him stumble; the rod was torn from between his legs, and blows rained on him where the one who had captured it struck him with it.

Then the milling crowd turned away from him, and he found enough strength to trudge away, back up the hill, a forlorn and wounded figure, no longer needed.

Star Blanket made his way south to the little creek in the timber, where he removed the ceremonial head, and the hooves and tail, and lowered himself into the water, weary yet triumphant, for now the buffalo would come and there would be meat for everyone, and warm robes to sleep in, and hides to trade for the white man's goods.

Pride helped him walk the final mile to his pony's hiding place in a grove of stunted cedars, and he rode home through the pale, golden twilight. No one was there to greet him, and he broke his fast with cold food from the kettle.

Weakened from his ordeal he crawled into his bed, falling promptly into a deep sleep, and was awakened only by the clatter made by Magpie when she entered the lodge and built up the fire. Soon Grass Heart and her father came in. Star Blanket was sitting up, his chest thrust out. Good Plume gave him a civil grunt, but the girl merely scowled when she saw him.

He was deeply humiliated when his performance failed to bring the buffalo, and his spirit altogether shattered after being called to a meeting with White Cow and the other old chiefs. They berated him, some grumbling he had cheated in his fasting or prayers, and one voiced suspicions that he had not had his heart thoroughly in his performance, citing as evidence that he had too easily let the women take the red painted penis from him and that it proved him a weakling, a coward, and implied impotence.

"You do not deserve the name of warrior," the old man charged, and they allowed him no words in his defense.

Then his disgrace was completed when friends of Grass Heart visited the lodge and she confided in them that the Buffalo Spirit had been no more inspired in his copulations than was her husband, at which Good Plume laughed immoderately and the women tittered behind their hands.

Running outside, he kicked her dog and spit on the doorpost paintings, watching with rage the liquid run down the wings of a butterfly, staining them. But it dried quickly and the picture looked as fresh as ever.

Desperate from his failure he set out to hunt alone, and in a thicket of buffalo berries, its red fruit beginning to ripen, wasps stirring the leaves in a fury of greed, he met with an old-woman bear. She struck him dead with one swipe of her juice-covered hand.

When his horse returned without him, a search party was sent out. Good Plume rode with them in spite of his bad knee; it was very painful and he was forced to use a series of stacked logs to mount. It began to rain, lightly, as they trailed downriver through the little draws and canyons that led into it. In one of them they found the body; it lay among wet grass. The face was missing and mice had removed the brains.

They brought him home. Grass Heart and Magpie sewed him in his robes and they took him to a secret place in the woods where they placed the body in the fork of a tree. Others rested there, a secluded, ghostly tribe of the dead, and Grass Heart shivered when she heard the soft rain drip on the leaves like the tapping of bony fingers.

She had refused to mourn him as a wife, but Magpie halfheartedly gashed her arms and legs and put a film of ashes on her face and hair, apprehensive that now her brother was gone she would be made to return to her parent's lodge. She need not have worried: she had become indispensable to Good Plume's comfort, and also Grass Heart's, and nothing was ever spoken of her rejection, but through a few significant looks between the two, an agreement was made without words. She remained with them, but not for as long as expected.

⌒

IT WAS EARLY MORNING, and the July sun, as large around and as bright as her father's shield, shone down on the cornfields and on Grass Heart's head.

The river was still and brown, a path between the trees. In the village the children were listless in the shadows, and up on the prairie the horse herds crowded under the trees along its borders, sweat funneling their hides and flies hooding their eyelids. Dogs drowsed in the lodges, snarling in their sleep.

Grass Heart laid down her hoe when she heard the boat whistle below the big bend of the river. The sound echoed from the cliffs, and the cannon of the fort boomed in answer. She looked at Magpie, who never ceased hoeing, her head bent over her bone tool, and shrugged her shoulders.

She had come to the garden at Magpie's insistence. In her clumsiness she had dug up too many of the smaller plants and was leaning on her hoe, staring at the puffs of dirt flying from her sister-in-law's slow steady movements. Magpie was an excellent gardener, so much so that Good Plume had entrusted his tobacco plot to her that summer. Her sister, Rabbit Ear, had helped in the cornfield, but now sat in the brush-covered arbor with a group of women who were resting from their labors. Their moccasins lay on the ground, and they were waving their feet in the hot air, laughing noisily.

One of them nudged Rabbit Ear and pointed toward Grass Heart. "I wouldn't let her in *my* field," she said, "she would put a curse on it."

"I don't eat none of hers," Rabbit Ear replied. "She don't work anyway, just stands around."

"Don't sweat, either," the other quipped and they all giggled and peered at the far figure.

Grass Heart had seen the pointing finger and knew they were discussing her. She could see in her mind their greasy cheeks, their dirty feet, and could almost smell their sweat. She wiped at her own forehead with her sleeve.

The boat churned up the river and after much effort docked at the fort, its wake rocking her own small craft where it floated in the green shade of the trees.

In boredom she wandered down to where the bullboats lay beached and pushed her own out into the sluggish stream. She used the carved paddle to swing out into the current and let it carry her downstream. A huge turtle crossed before her, his wrinkled head cleaving the water. His fierce beak reminded her of her father. In the marsh to the west of her, crested heron fed; they raised their long necks above the reeds; the sunlight on their feathers made them gleam like brass. Half-asleep, she dug her paddle into the muddy shallows, tied the rope from her boat to it, and sat there, thinking of nothing.

A white man, stationed mid-river in a canoe, watched her out of sight. He was anchored there, pretending to fish, his eyes on the village across the way.

Mr. Knipp had ordered him there. "Act like you are fishing," he had said.

"It ain't natural," he had protested. "There's no fish around here and none going to bite this time of day even if they was. I'm goin' to look like a damned fool."

"Then you'll look like usual," the agent snapped. "Do as I say."

The heat crumpled his scalp under the soft hat he wore, and his shirt was drenched with sweat. The reflection of the sun from the water burned his eyes, and he rubbed at them constantly, keeping in mind the task that had been set him, and the promised bottle of whiskey from Mr. Knipp. He was to turn back any boats that left the village and crossed toward the fort.

It proved impossible to carry out; while he managed to send back several, four others swept past him, and he tallied the number of people in them on the paper he had been given. Vaguely he felt the explanation for his job had been unsatisfactory. It was to be a census of how many of the Mandan wished to trade on the first day a boat came.

"If you can't stop them, count them," the agent had said. He was arguing heatedly with a bullboat containing four women and a man, so he missed altogether Grass Heart's slow progress as she pushed her boat upstream close to the eastern shore.

JAKE MOON HAD BEEN FEELING SICKLY all morning, and as soon as they docked at Fort Catherine he pushed his way through the crowd of Indians at the foot of the gangplank and made his way to the trade room where he found a clerk he remembered from the year before and to whom he entrusted his few belongings.

"You sick?" the clerk inquired, looking closely at him, then backing off and dropping the rope-tied bundle. His expression was wise and alarmed. "Go away," he told Jake.

He went to the back pasture, looking for Posey, his legs moving as light as water. She was feeding, her rat-colored rump high in the air. A steady grinding of her square teeth made him smile. He pulled her head up with an unsteady hand, saying, "I've come back." She peered at him in her round-eyed way, and he let her go and walked to the stables. There, he found an empty stall, cool and dark, and soon forgot where he was or why he had come.

ON BOARD THE *ST. PETER* Mr. Knipp was shouting furiously, his men shoving and cursing the Indians who had clambered onto the deck.

"Off! Off!" he bellowed, hatless, and brandishing a huge pistol in the air. Suddenly he fired it, the sound reaching the man in the canoe.

"Hear that? Mr. Knipp means it, you can't come nigh the boat till he says!" he told the Indians arguing with him. Without another word they turned their boats and left him, flailing back to shore. Breathless with relief, he picked up the fishing pole he had laid in the bottom of the canoe, and settled back.

"The sun will kill me afore the Indians kin," he said aloud.

Grass Heart's craft lay under the swell of the *St. Peter*'s bow, unseen from above. The pistol shot made her jump and she almost lost her grip on the side of the boat. Her hand had been feeling the name painted on its prow. The letters had been carelessly done, and their crooked shape had teased her into touching. The sudden crack of the gun startled her, and she sat down abruptly, her small boat swinging outward. Mr. Knipp stood directly over her, his jaw sliding up and down above his swollen neck.

Indians milled about ashore where they had run or jumped from the boat in some disorder at the agent's shot. These were the beggar Indians who lived near the fort in teepees copied from those of the Sioux, but much smaller, made of untanned hides that smelled dank, or in brushy lodges they threw up to sleep in. They spent their days beneath the trees where they camped, or squatting alongside the wall of the fort, in the sun when the cold winds blew and in the shade when the sun burned down. They took great enjoyment from the white men's activities and traded with them whatever they owned or could steal for the whiskey that made them fall over like dead men, no one caring so long as they stayed peaceful, their wives sharing their pleasures and their daughters docilely following the white men into the bushes.

Grass Heart had always believed that Mr. Knipp's tolerance of them was evil, that he should send them away instead of letting them hang about the fort, for their true business was meant to be buffalo hunting, and horse stealing, and war parties.

She had never dared say so, but she thought the last two ridiculous pursuits, especially the war parties, with all the fuss of purification and fasting, and the elaborate decorations painted on the war horses and the men themselves, a waste when one considered how long it took to gather the roots and berries for the desired colors, and the slow cooking that made them possible.

And if the men were fortunate, they came home with some scrawny animals they immediately gave away to prove their good hearts, and bloody scalps off some unfortunate enemies, acting over-proud. Then they gave those things to their women to hang on hoops. They danced with them, shrieking and shaking them in the smoky air, like trophies of great value.

That snatching of hair—all it did was encourage the men. They boasted and bragged too much for her taste. She was very thankful Good Plume had given up scalp hunting while she was yet in her childhood, for she had seen too many warriors brought back to the village slung over a horse like a slain deer, either wounded or dead. And if the man was killed, all the women in his family were made to cut off their hair and gash their arms and legs with knives, until one could almost hear the blood splashing in their moccasins as they walked by. No wonder white men called them savages! she thought.

And now there was Mr. Knipp standing just over her, shouting. She stared at his red face.

"Get out of here!" he howled. "Don't you hear me? I told you, get away, go home, don't come this side of the river again!"

She was so astonished she could not speak. She sat there, her mouth hanging open, shocked.

"Get the hell home!" he screeched, and she turned her boat and paddling furiously went home to tell her father.

⌐

MR. KNIPP HAD SURPRISED HIMSELF with his vehement orders to Grass Heart and shaded his eyes to see her as she passed the man in the canoe.

He had taken what precautions he could, seeing the Indians chased away from the *St. Peter,* and after giving orders to the pilot, he left for his office. A priest was waiting for him there, and with no hesitation the agent drew out a stone jug from under the table and offered him a drink.

Father Bernard kept his gentle gray eyes fastened on Mr. Knipp, marveling at the smooth long swallows the man made as he drank. The agent drew a rather dirty handkerchief from his pocket and wiped daintily at his lips and mustache and said, "Would you perhaps care for water, or maybe some tea?" His voice carried little civility; the priest's presence was a nuisance; he did not want him in his fort. For that matter, he wished to see no one. His intention was to lower, considerably, the contents of the jug.

The priest stood, waiting. A small, black-clad man, he was displeased with the agent's drinking, but his round face showed nothing of how he felt.

"How did he board?" Mr. Knipp demanded. "Didn't anyone see what was wrong?" And he lifted the jug once more.

It reminded Father Bernard of his sister's trouble, even to the dabbing with the handkerchief; although she used her sleeve and sometimes her bare arm, or the hem of her dress, the exaggerated gesture having in it more of defiance than gentility.

"The poor lad was all right, then. He said he was going to Fort Union, too, a new clerk for the company. He did look ill but not so as to cause anyone to question him. He died in the night, a sad time for anyone when among strangers. Did it quietly."

Mr. Knipp found himself studying the man's bare, sunburnt head. It leaned to the left, slowly, as if to drop on his shoulder, and he felt his own tipping slightly and tore his gaze away.

"I have told the captain not to unload anything, but to pull out at once," he said. "I suspect some of the crew are already infected." The jug gurgled as he lifted it, and a little breeze through the open window ruffled his hair. He sighed. "And those Indians! There was no way to keep them off, short of shooting them. They are sure to take it."

"I have learned," the priest murmured, "that they will pick up anything not securely fastened down."

It took Mr. Knipp a moment to realize the little man was speaking seriously, for he continued: "Minor thievery is a problem all along the river. The men on board complained they were missing several personal articles wherever we stopped for wood and Indians got on the vessel."

He rubbed his cheeks absently and said, "I will stay to help, I have had the disease."

"I can't let you do that," Mr. Knipp exclaimed. "I have already arranged for horses and men to take you on to Fort Union."

The priest shook his head; his pink crown caught a sunbeam, lighting it. It made a faint halo about it, and the agent, liquor warming his heart, thought idly of angels, and put the jug under the table.

No matter how hotly Mr. Knipp argued, Father Bernard closed his ears to his words, and Knipp left him after the cook brought a bowl of water and a cloth with which to wash, glancing back to see him merrily slopping water about. A blackbird in a puddle, he thought grumpily.

Angels and birds? He thought it best not to drink any more that day and went out to see the *St. Peter* leave for downriver. His thirst remained, but he worked diligently at his papers until Father Bernard fetched him out to see the sunset.

"I am mad for sunsets," Father Bernard said, and Mr. Knipp found himself shuddering. He thought the priest absurd.

At the table that night the little man laid down his knife and pushed away his plate, saying, "I baptized him, without his permission."

"Yes," said Mr. Knipp. His hands were not steady, nor his appetite good. The stone jug was empty. "We should see to it," he said.

In a shed next to the stables they stood over the body lying on a plank. "He already smells," said the agent.

"In bad odor," the priest whispered.

Mr. Knipp laughed nervously, until he saw how solemn was the man's face. "Hold the lantern steady," he was ordered, but found it a strain, for the cloth he held over his nose kept slipping downward. Father Bernard began sprinkling water from a small bottle, flinging it about liberally while speaking in a strange tongue. When he had finished they each took an end of the plank and carried it out into the night.

The moon was shadowed by flimsy clouds and gave just enough light to see by. They chose a spot next to a horse trough where the moist earth was easily dug. Mr. Knipp had earlier placed shovels beside the stable door, and they set to work, a shallow grave neatly finished before he realized it. Lowering the corpse into the hole, they then layered the dirt back, and the agent removed himself to a respectful distance while the priest finished his mysterious rites.

The flat dark figure standing against the rolling moonlit pasture gave Knipp an eerie feeling; he found he was cold in spite of the hot night. He still held the lantern, leaning against the wall of the stable, thinking of tomorrow.

"Life is a dream," he said aloud and suppressed a belch.

"Done," a voice said in his ear and he dropped the lantern.

"Never mind, it was out anyway," Father Bernard said when he bent to lift it up. Mr. Knipp had not noticed.

He set the shovels and lantern inside the stable door and when he was safe in his room he drank himself into strange dreams and nightmares.

⌒

THE SAME MOON GAVE LIGHT to the path that led from Black Deer's doorway in the village. He stepped out from his lodge into its silvered light, anticipation carrying him quickly along the street. He adjusted his fine red blanket around his shoulder; his love whistle, dangling from a thong tied to his braid, clicked against the bone necklace around his throat.

He knew he was one of the richest, bravest warriors of all the Mandan, but he had a wife with a tongue like a snake's. This night she had been sweet-tempered and spoke nicely to him. Even her mother had given him a reluctant smile and an extra chunk of meat, and brought out her hoarded sugar, letting him spoon as much as he wanted into coffee.

Black Deer had risen before dawn and was waiting below the big bend when the *St. Peter* steamed by. He had clambered over the side and tied his bullboat to the railing and sought out the man he had dealt with before.

They made a hasty bargain, his mink skin for a length of red flannel. The man he traded with acted queerly, insisting on making the exchange where none saw them, then made Black Deer conceal the cloth under his shirt. He was suspicious and thought the cloth might have been stolen, and did as the man said. Quietly he slipped over the rail and set out for home, well satisfied, the cloth wrapped in a piece of deerskin in the bottom of his boat. He rowed gently, so as not to spill water over the side.

His wife, Her Enemy, exclaimed happily over his gift to her and praised him for it, properly awed at his cunning in the trade. It blunted her criticism of him when he left her and went off to the river to bathe and spend his afternoon visiting friends after greasing his hair and dressing in his new shirt.

After showing the bundle of cloth to all her family members she hurried off to her friends, bearing the bright length over her arm.

And she was still good-natured that evening, not scolding the children as they ate. Black Deer rummaged for his love whistle; he found it at last in a doeskin pouch hanging in the rear of the lodge among bags of dried sage and prairie turnips. The mother-in-law held the baby on her hip, bending to the fire, when he crept past, his blanket hidden under his far arm.

Once outside he went with stately tread to the lodge of Seven Birds, where the girl came at once to the sound of his mournful whistle and let him take her into his blanket. Her hair smelled of sweet grass smoke as he laid his eager face against it. He was dazzled with love. He had chosen her to be his second wife, and she would accept him.

He held her closer and bit her gently on the ear, at the same moment as Jake Moon, across the silvered river, came awake when the voice said "DONE."

It came from the wall next to his ear. He lifted his head and vomited down the front of his best shirt, turned on his stomach and threw up into his new second-hand hat, rolled to one side and soiled his only trousers. He felt he was dying.

"I am not done yet," he said, but fell unconscious and did not know what happened after that.

⌐

FATHER BERNARD DID NOT SLEEP AT ALL that night, and when dawn appeared, scarlet in the east, he was standing on the riverbank, listening to the earth awaken, his morning prayers long over.

Grouse whistled in the long grass on the hillsides. River birds skimmed the still dark water. It promised another day of oppressive heat, and he breathed deeply of the fresh, cool air.

A few Indians came stumbling from their huts, naked, or else clutching a bit of cloth about their loins, girls timidly stepping through the rough grass knowing his eyes were on them, the men and women silent and deliberate.

It always amazed the priest that these people bathed each day no matter the season, even breaking the ice in winter and plunging in, a thing no sensible white man would ever consider doing.

A girl sang as she splashed in the shallows, her body sparkling as the sun's first rays touched the water. He watched her, humbled by her natural affinity with the rich liquid, the soft morning air, shadowed into blue and purple beneath the overhanging trees, and the resplendent sky pearled with pink that blushed her skin and caught in her hair.

She stumbled and for a moment stood upright, then fell face down, and he ran to her and lifted her up, his black skirts floating on the water.

Afterwards, when he thought about it, it seemed to him her body had begun to swell while still in his arms, and as he laid her on the grass her skin blackened.

⟿

GRASS HEART HAD DRAWN HER BOAT UP onto the grassy verge, her face flushed with anger. Ignoring the shouts of friends calling her to go berry picking, she ran to her lodge and was calling her father before she was over the threshold.

Good Plume was not there. Magpie was also gone, and she stood in the dim room stamping her feet in frustration. A moccasin flew off and she removed the other and hurled it in the fire. Ranting, she paced about, but with no one to hear her it had no edge. She consoled herself by digging through her ornaments, her wrath declining as time passed, until she seated herself and began to question why Mr. Knipp had appeared so enraged, and why he had shouted so rudely at her. Clearly there was something she did not understand and that had caused his extraordinary behavior.

It had something to do with the boat, she decided, something he did not wish her to know of or to become involved in. It went far beyond his enforcement of Good Plume's rule that she was forbidden to go to the fort unless he accompanied her, and she puzzled over it.

Do I tell my father or don't I? Does he know anything about it? Do I wait until he speaks? She thought it wiser to wait.

Good Plume came late in the afternoon. He had been in council. He said they had learned the Sioux had moved away from the river to the higher prairies to the west, and the men were planning a buffalo hunt.

She listened impatiently, and when he ventured nothing else she served him his meal. After she had eaten too, she got out a bit of needlework, laying it aside before one row was finished. Magpie dropped an iron spoon into the kettle. The clang startled Grass Heart and she yelled at the woman.

"There's no need to be so nasty," Magpie told her and put her flat, broad nose in the air and left to visit her sister. "Someday you will learn that other people have feelings too," she said at the door.

Good Plume peered curiously at his daughter, noting her mood, cleared his throat and remarked that she was as jumpy as a mouse. "What is wrong with you?" he asked.

"Ahhh," she said and cracked her knuckles. "There's some trouble at the fort."

He continued to smoke his pipe. Long shadows crept up the earthen walls toward the smokehole where the sky showed as round and blue as a white man's eye.

"Mr. Knipp was angry and they threw the Indians from the camp off the boat that came up today. He was terrible to me, told me to go home. He cursed, too." She watched him anxiously but could not read his face.

"I thought maybe the whites had gone to war with the Sioux again and didn't want any Indians from here to know about it." The sudden falsehood had jumped into her head, and she spoke it easily, knowing how the subject of warring on the Indians upset him.

Predictably, he launched into speech. "I have heard nothing of it, but it is quite possible. Those white men are always warring with someone, somewhere; they seem uncomfortable unless they are fighting." He warmed up and struck his bad knee with his fist, flinching. "They even fight one another. I heard that on my travels. And when they talked about war it was never of losing but of winning, and if they couldn't win they declared truces and made new weapons and fought again. It is pitiful to hear them! It would go much smoother for us if they placed less importance on winning and fought only until it got too dark, or too cold, or too hot. There's any number of reasons to stop fighting!"

He paused a moment, then said sadly, "It's a wonder there are any of them left, they fight so often. And they always win, so they say. I don't know about those battles they wage among themselves, who wins. It's always the same, though, with us. No sense of proportion."

He arose and scraped out the bowl of the redstone pipe with a twig, yawning. "Tomorrow I will go to the fort and find out what is wrong."

"But Mr. Knipp said to stay away," she said.

"Mr. Knipp has nothing to say where I can go or can't. No little agent who spends his days cheating our people and hiding his nose in a bottle tells Good Plume what he can do. He is here only by our consent, remember."

"Don't go," she said, alarmed. "Listen. You are getting old; it's hard for you to travel with your crippled leg. Don't get mixed up in their troubles."

He laughed at her, and with a horrible scowl she went with her stool to the doorway and sat there with her back to him.

Good Plume had intended to take her fishing the following day, to the upper reaches of the Knife River, for catfish. On his way out of the council house, he had stopped to examine the sky for weather, the sunset splashing red streaks across the sky. He had no cares on his mind and stood in the clearing before the lodge thinking of nothing in particular when old Hoop Feather came up to him and greeted him. Good Plume avoided looking directly at his face, for the old man had suffered some kind of affliction that had drawn one side of it down, the eye and mouth crooked and drooping. He spoke, with much spittle and slurring of words, of the sky, saying he hoped for rain, his wife's garden was drying from lack of it, then passed on into the lodge.

There he told the other men, who had come to smoke their pipes and visit, about the cunning of his son-in-law in sneaking onto the boat and measured out for them with arms spread three times the length of the flannel he had traded for, and how Her Enemy would divide it so that he would have enough to trim his good shirt with, and the men all joined in with approving "Ho's."

꩜

NOW, FEELING RATHER SILLY, Good Plume made sure his daughter, Grass Heart, and the slave, Magpie, were sleeping before he rose in the dark and carried the bundle he had ready out the door. He stood on the porch, making certain of the moon's position over the wall of trees across the river. It told him that half the night was done, and furtively he slipped through the streets to the rear of the village, where he edged over the fence into the deep ditch beyond, sliding silently in the soft dirt. The only guards were stationed in the gardens, now the Sioux were gone, and he evaded them by going up the sloping hillside. He made his way to that part of the river where the boulders were strewn about, careful of them, threading his way to the lower shore. He stopped there to rest.

The air was still and held the day's heat. Myriad sounds filled the night; he identified those of the insects and small animals and listened intently to the cry of a coyote, quickly answered by others. Their song was faint and pure, each note rising as though pulled upward by an invisible string to its ultimate, only to be released and fall, note by note, back to earth. A big-footed rabbit feeding in the lush grass at the water's edge startled him by its sudden flying leap as it fled to the thickets, and he laughed to himself.

Stepping through shallows until the river reached his knees, he slid into the water, his bundle atop his head, barely a ripple to show his passage. He swam soundlessly to the far shore. There he lay on the sand, panting a little, mildly amused at himself. I am pretending to be a warrior once more, pursued by enemies, or a horse stealer bent on thieving, he thought, smiling, then sobered.

Grass Heart couldn't accuse him of rashness, at least. Until he knew what had happened at the fort he would continue his cautious approach.

He climbed the high cliff to the east, pausing often, for his crippled knee hampered him. On the far side of the hill the sun was pushing over the horizon through a long high band of purpled clouds, yellow shafts from between them reaching to the flanks of the prairie. Finding a hollow in the rocks, he slept awhile, and when he awoke his knee had stiffened and he was forced to drag his leg as he crept along the north rim. He found it impossible to squat when he wished to look down on the fort, and running was but a memory.

The sun grew high, glancing off the rocks and blinding him. Soon he reached the place where the cliff fell away and a sharply tilted hill lay below, the pastures belonging to the fort beginning there. Painfully he lowered himself and peered down at the fort. He watched for a long time before rising and moving down.

He had seen figures along the wharf and in the courtyard, but none where the Indian camp stood. The lack of activity there puzzled him. Many of the people slept during the middle of the day, but others always could be found in the shade, mending boats or swimming under the trees. Looking closer he saw their tents and brushy huts were gone, and nothing remained of them but blackened circles in the grass.

His first thought was that the white men had killed them and burned all traces of their dwellings. But there would have been an alarm raised that would have been heard in the village directly across the river, and smoke and flames that would have alerted the guards in the gardens.

The horses in the pasture ran away at the sight of him, and he entered a back door of the stables without being seen or accosted. He poked about, finding nothing of interest. A narrow door led out into the courtyard and he stepped through it, stopping abruptly. A white man stood there.

"Where the hell did you come from?" he said. He was a squat fellow with eyes like plum pits. "You've no business here!" he shouted.

Good Plume regarded him stonily. He was one of those little white men who felt it necessary to use a big voice. "I came to see Mr. Knipp."

"Can't. Can't no Indian see him," the man said and started to speak again, but Good Plume interrupted him.

"He will see me."

Then he recognized the man who had hung the door on his lodge.

Another man came from a porch nearby. "He don't want to see nobody," he said and spat. "He seen enough of you Indians."

"Tell Mr. Knipp I am here."

"Don't you talk back to us, you ol' son of a bitch!" the first man shouted and raised his arm.

"Let him go, he ain't goin' far," said the other, scratching at his crotch. His trousers were too small and he had a rash there. It excited him.

Good Plume found the agent seated on a bench under a tree by the river, his head wrapped in a white cloth. He gave the Indian a slow nod, then bent to a pail on the ground beside him and wet the cloth, placing it back on his brow.

"What do you want?" he said.

"Where are our people?" Good Plume demanded.

The agent gestured with a shaking hand toward the river. "Most are gone," he said. His voice was vague and the pungent smell of whisky hung about him.

Good Plume looked on the agent with distaste as he began to mumble, catching the words "doom" and "death" and demanded once more an answer to his question. Mr. Knipp continued daubing his head and talking to himself. Letting himself down, his back against the tree trunk, Good Plume waited.

It was true, what Grass Heart had told him: the agent was hiding something, something he feared.

An old building once used as an icehouse stood back under a group of elm trees, and the two men came from it, walking toward them. He sensed their eyes on him and set his jaw.

"What's it like in the village?" Mr. Knipp spoke through his white cloth. "How many dead?"

At first Good Plume did not catch the meaning of his words, then awkwardly got to his feet, turning to flee, but the agent reached out and caught his arm. "You can't go," he said. They struggled briefly, and the agent called out sharply to the men who ran to help him, catching Good Plume from behind.

When he reached for his knife he found it gone. By then it did not matter. They led him to the old shed beyond the trees.

One man lifted down the bar across the door and opened it. A white man, wearing a black dress, his head bald and pink-colored, stood there as he was shoved within. Mr. Knipp had lost his white cloth and Good Plume saw his red, swollen eyes. He had been weeping.

The door slammed shut and those outside dropped the heavy wooden plank into place, the thud it made no louder than the beating of Good Plume's heart.

"What is this place?" he asked.

"A pesthouse," the other said. Pausing a moment, a bar of sunlight from a narrow window falling across his rosy skull, he regarded the old Indian with calm eyes.

"Smallpox," he said, and moved off into the darkness.

⌒

BLACK DEER FELL AGAIN, this time near the dead coals in the fire pit. His head thundered with the beating of drums; flames consumed his body. One out-flung hand lay on the still corpse of Her Enemy, the other scrabbling at the arrows he had been sharpening and dropped when his vision was lost.

The children no longer whimpered in their beds, the grandmother lying silent somewhere in the lodge, where he had pressed a robe over her face to stifle her cries. The old father had disappeared and he knew not where.

The beautiful red flannel cloth had carried Death. He gave it to his wife. She and the old mother passed it among the village women. His children had brought it to their friends for a game of hoop-a-stick. The crook-mouth old man took it with him to the council lodge and Seven Birds laid it with her narrow fingers into the kettle of soup.

His hand knew the arrows and he grasped one by the shaft, willing it to his throat.

⏤

FOR THE WHOLE DAY Grass Heart crouched in a terror-ridden mindlessness, her ears stuffed with moss, the door bolted shut.

She had awakened when someone shouted. Magpie was running about the lodge beating her head on the posts and moaning. When Grass Heart stood up from her bed the slave clutched her, then shoved her away and resumed her frenzied running, unable to speak. Suddenly she threw open the door and rushed into the street, and when the girl followed her she heard the shrieking and saw Death strike down the people.

She closed herself in, locked the door, and retreated to the rear of the lodge. Only then did she notice her father's absence.

The day passed, agonizingly slow; the smoke hole turned green, then dark blue, then black, silvered when the quarter moon rode through. Grass Heart took the ladder used to store things on the rafters and placed it against a round post, climbing upward. With her knife she hacked a hole through the earth and close-woven branches of the dome, until she had made an opening large enough to clamber through onto the roof. She sat on the sloping side and waited for dawn.

The hills to the east held back the sun, but its light touched those to the west, the corn-colored grasses bending in the soft morning breeze. Long shadows lifted like fog from the river bottom; the stream coiled around the cliffs to the south in a great half circle; she held her breath in horror.

A woman had stumbled from a lodge just below, lay down on her back and looked into the sky. A man followed her. He wore a wolf skin robe, one shoulder bare, his hair tied up with raven feathers. He was singing his death song, holding a child under each arm, a baby dangling by a leg circled by his fist. Gouts of blood spurted from its mouth, the man's mouth a black hole in his bulging face. The lament rose eerily above the other screams, piercing Grass Heart's spirit with limitless sorrow.

While she watched he threw the children to the ground, next to the woman. A knife flashed as he lifted it. He stabbed the children, as though crazed, until he stiffened, his arm upraised and his head flung back, and thrust the knife into his own breast, falling atop them.

A flock of crows came coasting from the woods, dropping into the corn-fields. Their faint screeching mingled with the cries and screams of the village. Grass Heart looked at the Death below and hid again in her lodge.

The following day she dared once more to climb to her spy hole. The family of the previous day still lay in the street. A pack of camp dogs was worrying the bodies, the baby half-devoured.

A different sound caught her attention and she saw a group of people lurching along a path near the rear gate, a ragged row with an old man leading them. He bore a long pole, the figure of Okeedah swaying from its end. It wore new clothing and had been freshly painted; straw stuffing dangled from its sleeves. His cap was crooked on the eyeless head, a black spotted face below it. The mob of singing, weeping people climbed the hill and passed from sight. She recognized many of them, but none was her father.

That night she made a hasty search for him and for Magpie, not daring to enter any of the lodges, just slipping through the streets, untended torches and cooking fires her only light. The horrors she saw sent her flying back to her lodge, sickened almost to death.

⤸

WHEN THE DOOR WOULD NOT OPEN when he shouted, Good Plume beat on it with his fists.

"Stop that. It will do no good," the little white man said.

Good Plume looked around. The room was low and dark, a stench filling it that made his eyes water. The bar of sunlight from the window picked out an arm, a sprawl of black hair, half a face, its eyes opening and closing in spasms. He went to the bare plank beds along the walls and looked down at the bodies lying on them. Some were covered with new pustules, white as paint against the dark skin. Others had open sores, their limbs distended until it seemed they would burst. The priest stood next to one, a stained cloth in one hand, a bucket in the other, holding a head that had little resemblance to a head, the mouth retched, and a yellow mucous dribbled from it.

The men had thrown his bundle in before barring the door, and Good Plume retrieved it. He lay his cheek against the open window, the iron bar cool against his skin, and took shallow gasps. I am in a prison, he told himself, and a growing rage heated his skin.

Good Plume knew about smallpox. He had seen it in Fort Atkinson when he journeyed with two other Mandan chiefs downriver during a time of peace. Few whites died of it, and the agent there had told him of the magic needle with which the doctors imposed the sickness on them. He had thought it a foolish way to practice medicine. But the Indian people had no defenses against the disease.

Outside, the river flowed, a rusty color from the sunset. He could see only that stretch of it that ran between the fort and the village; by shading his eyes the dimly rounded forms of the lodges stood out above the far shore and he searched for any signs of life there. The black skirt appeared next to him. "I am Father Bernard," the priest said. "Let us sit down."

They sat, side by side, where the air was freshest, Good Plume's profile sharp against the red sky. "So. Why am I here?"

"Mr. Knipp is trying to keep the sickness from spreading." He did not say how futile it was and wished he could see the sunset. It promised to be spectacular.

Weariness loosened the priest's bones; he wanted badly to sleep but denied himself. First there had been the quick-dead to bury, in holes scarcely deep enough to be called graves. There had been too many of them, and finally men from the fort with gloves on their hands dragged other bodies to the riverbank, where they shoved them into the water, under cover of darkness. He had helped to burn the huts and their contents, while Mr. Knipp separated those who appeared well from the sick.

Of the men in the fort, those who had not had smallpox were placed in a room, tended by those who had. There were not many of either distinction, and some who claimed they were immune stole horses from the herds and rode off the first night. Mr. Knipp at first refused any help for the Indians, saying they would die anyway. At some cost, the priest had finally been granted the use of the old shed.

The agent complained bitterly. The height of the fur-trading season was on, and his company expected him to increase the number of furs taken in from those of the previous year. Now he could not fulfill his contract. He would be replaced, and he railed against his fate.

Father Bernard kept his thoughts to himself; he found several men willing to help him, and they built the bunks and strengthened the door, placing iron slots on each end for the heavy plank that locked it from outside. It shut him in, and his fear of closed places made him sweat. Mr. Knipp sent food and water, and promised to do so every day, and arranged for removal of the dead. Father Bernard was to signal with a white cloth on a stick through the window.

After the heat of the day, fat green flies, drawn by the stench of the rotting bodies, settled on the two men, and they got out their pipes and tobacco pouches and the priest made a spark with his flint. They smoked, the gray plumes twinning together into one.

Good Plume was uneasy: he had no wish to spend the night with a dead spirit searching the low room for a way out, and asked, "If one dies, is he left in here?"

The priest shook his head. "No, men come to remove them." He stared at his feet. His boots needed patching.

"Are you from the village across the river?" he asked.

So Good Plume explained how he had left there in the darkness, knowing nothing of the sickness at the fort, knowing only that his daughter was disturbed. "I should have taken her advice," he said. "Here I am, imprisoned, sure to get the pox. She will never forgive me." The arch of his skull loomed against the square of sky behind him. He turned his face away. It had come to him he could die here, never to see her again, and his spirit turned upside down with sorrow.

Father Bernard was thinking of the dead youth, so hurriedly shoveled beneath the horse trough such a short time ago. The lad had whispered his name as he lay sick, and his pulse had grown feebler and stopped altogether in the shrunken wrist. He had held the young man as he moaned and gurgled, the gaping mouth drooling blood. How that death would change the world! Along with our greed we bring them disease and death and endow them with hate. It is nurtured by their spilled blood, entombs their hearts, rots virtue, destroys pride, honor, valor.

A whispered entreaty for water brought him from his somber thoughts; he hurried with a cup to a woman who could not swallow it. Soon after she gave a final gasp, and Father Bernard tied his white cloth to the stick and set it out the window. He stepped over the form of Good Plume, who seemed asleep, to watch the night breeze toss the flag against the sky. The moon crept along her lesser path. Nighthawks dipped silently above the river. He dreamt of home.

A hand clutched his ankle. "I am sick," Good Plume said, and vomited.

"Do you have a fever?" The priest touched his forehead, feeling the pustules forming. Then Good Plume passed into delirium.

He shouted and roared and bleated. With much difficulty the priest got him to a vacant bunk, but there was one desperate moment when the Indian got him by the neck and said, "I think I will kill you." His hold loosened and he struck out, his hand catching the dimly burning lantern that hung from the rafter, knocking it to the floor. The light went out.

"I am blind!" he shouted hoarsely and fell face down on the planks, his head hitting the wall. He lay quietly.

Father Bernard got the lantern going again and sank down by the door. He knew dawn was near; he waited for the men to come for the dead woman.

They were careless from lack of sleep; they left the door open. Good Plume sprang from his bed and leaped past them, running for the river, his crippled leg flying. He heaved himself into the water before they reached him.

The moon lay a band of silver across it and they could see his high skull riding on it. "Don't let him escape!" the priest bellowed, his skirts around his thighs. He ran after the men.

They fished him out. He did not fight them; rather he seemed dazed and allowed them to drag him to the pesthouse. On the dirt floor he lay shivering, watching as they lifted the dead Indian woman and carried her out, slung between them like a dead goat. The door was barred once more, its hollow thump echoing in the dawn. The frightened priest scolded him, his round face pale with exhaustion.

"You must not try to run away," he said, and to his astonishment the old man began to laugh.

"I feel quite well, now, and no longer stink. I believe I shall sleep awhile," Good Plume said and lay down on his bed and closed his eyes.

⌐

JAKE MOON RECOVERED. His legs were weak, but he walked without help from the sickroom of the fort to the pesthouse, at the insistence of Frankie Paradise.

"That little feller down there needs some help," he told Jake, "and since you is well enough to git around and you bein' a civilian, not hired like us other, Mr. Knipp says to show you where."

Jake did feel well, but for an unrelenting hunger, his belly never full enough to suit him, and he laid the blame on the two men in charge of the fort hospital, suspecting his food rations were held back and used by themselves. Their rounded, healthy-looking stomachs affronted him.

"Mr. Knipp never said anything to me about this," he said. "I don't care about nursing Indians any more than you."

"He ain't sayin' much to anybody, he's stayin' drunk in his room and we don't see him but once to awhile. But long as I'm runnin' this, I say you go." And Frankie smiled, evilly.

When the door of the shed was opened for him the terrible smell beneath the low roof smote him. A horrible nausea came over him. He felt his way through the gloom to an empty bed, an upper one, and lifted himself carefully into it, a corner of his shirt stuffed in his mouth. As he lay there, his eyelids quivering, a far different odor drifted upward to him and he leaned over to look for its source, fainting immediately and falling to the floor.

He opened his eyes to find an old Indian studying his face, his own so close to Jake's that he could make out each line creasing its skin, making him think of bird tracks in the mud.

"You stupid fool, you ruined my pipe! Why do you want to break my pipe!" and Good Plume picked it up and felt of it gently.

"Why are you lying on the floor?" asked the priest, coming up to them.

"He fell out of bed, trying to take my pipe," Good Plume grumbled. "Look at him, he has holes in his face!" He poked Jake in the ribs. "Come to the window so I can see it."

Jake wanted only to crawl back into his bunk and made a tentative attempt, but the old Indian drew him toward the light.

"Your luck was bad," he said. "I was sick too, but cured myself. And I did it alone. I have no scars, nothing, and I'll tell you why. I fell in the river!" He paused in triumph. "Yes, that is what happened, and I tell this priest to send word to the doctors just to put everybody in cold water when the fever comes on them. *It cures the pox!*"

Father Bernard intervened then with introductions, and looked faintly dismayed when Good Plume turned away at Jake's name, leaving the youth with open mouth and outstretched hand. Finally realizing the Indian was not turning back, Jake dropped his hand. If Grass Heart's father did not care to shake it, there was nothing he could do.

"He's a difficult man," whispered the priest, "don't let it worry you. And it's not true he has no pox marks, they are there all right, under the hair across his forehead, deep enough so they won't fade. Someday he'll look in a mirror and find them and he won't be quite so vain about his wonderful cure."

Jake had been shocked to learn his face was pitted, and when he felt no one was watching him he peered into the water pail near the window but saw only the murky liquid, leaves and twigs clouding its surface.

Father Bernard assured him later that he was healing nicely and that the scars would eventually disappear, since he was still young, but he suspected the priest of lying, and lay in his dark corner, brooding.

It rained that night; thunder and lightning filled the valley. It drew Jake from his bed and he joined the priest and the Indian at the window, where the lightning gave them glimpses of tossing trees and heaving water. The oil was low in the lamp and Father Bernard lit a candle, which the wind promptly extinguished. They spoke very little, the priest smoking his pipe, sharing his store of tobacco with Good Plume, who did not like its taste and added a bit of sage to it. Jake squatted against the wall, his hands folded on his knees, hearing the thunder's booming, the cool wet wind soothing him. His stomach churned with hunger. The smell of the pipe made him dizzy.

Father Bernard spoke of nothing in particular: how the river looked in moonlight; the time he had eaten buffalo ribs, broiled on a green wood fire, and how their richness had made him ill. He mentioned his family, speaking his sister's name, drawing out the final *ah* of it like a sigh. Good Plume caught the sadness behind it and peeked in surprise at him.

They were all three weary, needing sleep, but no one moved until the storm, its back to the river, pushed eastward over the hills, leaving raindrops to drum softly on the roof. Then with a great mutual yawning the men separated, going each in turn to their sleeping places, without words.

⌐⌐

ONE DAY A BOAT CAME UPRIVER. Its whistle was silent; it crept to the wharf with the least possible sound, the men aboard poling it to shore. Mr. Knipp was expecting it: a horseman had come upriver from Fort Pierre, riding by night and hiding by day, with an urgent message for the agent. He was to vacate the fort immediately. A boat was being sent for him and his men, and whatever materials and stores he could load aboard.

The news sent him from apathy to a frenzy of activity, and he blundered about giving orders, mainly ineffective since many were contradictory. Frankie Paradise was sent off with the horses, accompanied by a young fellow scarcely able to ride, let alone herd the animals, with orders to drive them to Fort Pierre. The two milk cows, beloved by the lanky cook, were shot and left to rot in the sun, the oxen driven out onto the prairie and left there, abandoned.

The clerks packed papers and ledgers and account books into sacks; the precious metal tallies with which the furs were tagged were crammed into a box that was overlooked and left behind. Clothing and utensils and personal effects were jumbled together, much of it forgotten in their haste, but Mr. Knipp secured his own bundles with strong rope and saw to it they were put aboard first when the boat arrived.

He left until the last hour his visit to Father Bernard, for he hoped to persuade the priest to leave with him, it being a matter of conscience, he told himself. He also recognized the element of self-interest. If he left the man behind, alone with the Indians and the vengeful feeling sure to arise from the epidemic, he himself would be blamed for whatever brutalities the priest would endure—torture, death—and Knipp darted from those realities like a mouse from a coyote, rehearsing his arguments as he walked to the pesthouse.

At his call, the small round face of the priest shone out between the bars of the window, and after lifting down the plank across the door the agent motioned him out.

For safety he brought along a burly woodcutter, armed with a rifle, who sat down under a tree nearby while the two men talked, his enormous hands busy with a knife. He whittled birds from the ash and poplar he selected from the woods, beautiful specimens that he returned to the timber, the birds in nests he fashioned from weeds and leaves set in the trees, a secretive act he hid from the others in the fort.

Mr. Knipp fidgeted with his mustache, motioning the priest to sit beside him on the bench beneath the elm. He wore his peacock vest, and it rippled and danced with each movement he made. The priest was bewitched by their colors.

"I've had my orders," Knipp said. "The fur company has closed their trading here. The fort is to be abandoned. You see, it was never made to be defended against the Indians here; they have always been peaceful enough. I'm afraid that is over now. And my usefulness here is ended. We are ready to leave, and you are to come too."

"Why, I cannot!" Father Bernard exclaimed, "not so long as there are sick ones still to be cared for."

The agent bent over his boot and tightened the strings, not wanting the flush that he felt rising in his face to be seen. Ordinarily he lied easily. Deceit was part of his profession, but it was somehow different to lie to the priest. Shame nibbled at him, momentarily.

"It wasn't just orders for me, and not just from my company. The government back in Washington wants us out of here, you included. No more missionary work in this part of the country. Your Bishop agreed. So. Off to your room. Gather up your things and be ready by the half hour." He rose briskly to his feet, sensing the other's distress. At that moment he almost liked the priest.

He had been more than a nuisance, showing up on the *St. Peter* with a dead boy whom he had been made to help bury under the horse trough, looking without pity at him when he cracked a badly needed jug to temper his troubles, hiding in his black cloth and weighing him with those gray eyes.

But the priest had taken over the pesthouse, freeing him from that duty, so he owed him something. He was repaying him by forcing him to come away, even at the cost of a lie. He gave the priest a clap on the back that rocked him dangerously and smiled.

"Then I have no choice," Father Bernard said finally. "I am obliged to obey my Bishop."

Mr. Knipp took him by the arm. "None of us have a choice."

He felt a twinge of pleasure at his success, then annoyance when the priest began to speak worriedly of the sick in the pesthouse. He promised enough food and water would be left for them for the next few days, saying "They can get water from the river soon enough, being on the mend now, and as for food an Indian can find it anywhere, you know that."

He called to the woodcutter, who was looking in the window of the hut, and taking a firm hold on Father Bernard's arm, he propelled him hurriedly off to the fort, forgetting his promise the instant they reached the gates.

Miles downriver he remembered, and shrugged it off. Then he was suddenly struck by a thought and tried to see, in his mind, whether the door to the pesthouse had been open or shut when he had left the bench with the priest. He was unable to picture it except with the plank in place. The image haunted him; he sought to dim it with drink, to Father Bernard's consternation. He knelt on the open deck next to his bedroll and offered up a prayer for him, after asking that special favors be granted to those poor souls left behind.

As for Mr. Knipp, he regaled the crew with bawdy songs in the cabin room and tried to imitate how the Indians danced, toppling over in mid-step and breaking into foolish tears.

The boat moved on, southward, between the black, arching trees that blotted out the starlight and the form of the moon.

⌒

GRASS HEART HAD SEEN THE BOAT when it came. She was leaning from her spy hole, her feet solid on the rafter below. Smoke from the vessel's stack trailed after it, a green-wood brown. No whistle called, no shouts or booming cannon. It stole to the wharf and stopped there and she could not see any more, it being too far away. When she looked the following morning it was gone.

Numb with disappointment she climbed down and notched another day on the doorpost, her eyes narrowed in the dim light, her hands trembling. The water jugs were empty, all but one, and she drank sparingly, then gnawed on a handful of dried corn. She returned to the notches. Her count had not been accurate and in confusion she studied them, going finally to the door where she lingered, fingering the lock. She turned it and stepped outside.

She was deaf to the sounds from the village, fewer and fainter now; they had become too common to move her, but she couldn't bring herself to walk the streets in bright sunlight and went back into the lodge to wait for night.

At dusk she was ready.

Camp dogs fed in the streets and she ran quickly past them, her head averted. A man sitting against a lodge appeared dead as she approached, but then she smelled the smoke from his pipe and saw the small mouth of fire in the bowl open and close. A pack of wolves, pale and swift, moved down a distant street, and the man's head turned toward them. He chose neither to see her nor to speak, and, holding her nose against the stench, she ventured farther into the center of the village, several times coming upon those like herself, alone in their terror. No one spoke: it was as if their tongues had grieved too long and lost the act of speech.

She returned to her lodge, locking the heavy door behind her, and with cold resolve planned her search for her father.

At daybreak she was ready, a pouch with food tied to her belt, her butcher knife in its beaded sheath tied to her leg just above the knee. In one hand she carried a long ash stick, the other holding the short double-edged spear that had been Good Plume's, a wicked instrument little used since his youth. With the last of her water she wet a handful of moss and stuffed her nose carefully, placing what moss was left over in the pouch with the food. She left the lodge without a backward look.

She barely glanced at those bodies she had encountered before; most of them were torn beyond recognition. Where she found the dead heaped together she poked gently among them with her stick, lifting deerskins and peering under robes and blankets. She was looking for a very tall, high-skulled corpse.

A white sun stood in the sky. Its heat pressed down. Along the shaded sides of the lodges dogs lay panting, their bellies distended. Gray wolves rested with them in friendly sprawls, their yellow eyes mild, and on the rooftops vultures and ravens teetered and croaked, making her quiver with loathing; she felt haunted and lowered her eyes.

In his lodge the Weather-Keeper lay naked on his stomach, great bubbles of gaseous flesh riding on his buttocks, the owl-prophet stalking back and forth along an outstretched arm.

She found She Sleeps under a robe in her lodge, lying on a raised platform where animals could not reach her. Rats had taken her fingers, but that was all, and Grass Heart uncovered her head and gazed on her face, as beautiful as ever, wondering what she had died of, then found the knife wound in her breast, hidden by a fold of her gown.

Man's Voice and his family sat along a wall, the eldest son down to the smallest girl, the three wives, in importance of their family ties, ranged alongside. All had great gashes in their throats. She was puzzled at first by the black lines that radiated down their faces and necks until she bent closer and saw them move, a long busy army of ants.

Dog Soldier had crushed the skull of his newborn with a rock he still held in his hand; he sat by his wife's body, crooning. His face was unmarked. His eyes were crazed, and Grass Heart hastily backed away from the doorway and continued her search.

She went to every lodge, and in almost each one scenes of horror met her. There were things about the madness, the bizarre behavior their occupants had exhibited when the epidemic struck, that she could not comprehend. The gruesomeness of it stunned her, and she went to sit in an empty, echoing dark porch until her senses returned.

The trail led over the prairie, marked by bones. The sun stole her sight, its brightness ominous, paling even the blue shadows under the trees. She followed the path marked by skeletons until there were no more, and swung to the south, to the little creek where she stopped to drink, retching wildly when she spied a child's legs floating among the moss, the half-seen body hidden beneath the green scum.

At the cliff beyond the gardens she paused long enough to survey what lay below. Then she climbed down the rocks. Skeletons lay scattered about among the boulders, and she read each skull with care. Most were crushed where the people had dashed themselves to their deaths, but again she found none like her father's. Shreds of rotten skin not yet plucked from the bones by the birds were draped over the rocks. Sated gulls and crows sat on the largest stones. They did not fly at her presence, their eyes heavy and full, and she screamed at them and beat at them with her long stick, some hopping away from it, only to settle back, humping their wings in unease.

A ring on a finger, a gaily beaded moccasin, brass bracelets and earrings. A scrap of blue cloth, long beads of rare shells, a cheek painted with a yellow circle. The short sparse braids tied with flowered calico, the long glossy braids bound with copper wire.

All these she put names to, spasms of despair shaking her like the fever sickness.

She had found bodies, but not her father's, Good Plume, and on the riverbank she rested, her head hanging between her knees.

The sun had moved far across the sky, concealed in a wall of dazzling clouds. There was nowhere else to search, nowhere but the fort, and she pitched forward, putting her sweated face in the water, letting it wash over her brow, her eyes, her cheeks, until it seeped into her mouth.

At last she roused herself and walked the shore, finding a bullboat. It had no paddle and she pushed it out onto the river. The day had deepened; the water ran bloody from the sunset. She set her course by the first star to the east. As she neared the far shore she saw deer drinking, and they wheeled to run, their white rumps flashing in the dusk. Prairie wolves began to sing; a horned moon came suddenly over the hill; a breeze curled along the broad path of the water.

The boat well concealed in a thicket, she climbed a friendly tree and in its fork she placed her pouch, her stick and spear, and with her back against the sturdy trunk, she slept. Once she woke. A bear snuffled beneath her on the forest floor, then was gone.

⌒

FATHER BERNARD HAD NOT RETURNED. Good Plume and Jake discussed in low tones what had happened to him but reached no agreement.

Good Plume sat at the window; he saw men carrying bundles and boxes to the wharf.

The light was poor and his eyes crossed with the strain. Jake Moon was repairing a broken slat in his bunk. When he finished he came to the window, crouched down, and crowded against the Indian, asking him what he saw. The old man refused to tell, saying instead, "Don't breathe on me like that any more, your mouth smells foul, the rest of you even more so."

Aggrieved, Jake drew back, and Good Plume, with a fling of his elongated head, went across to the other wall, pipe in hand. He suspected what all the furtive scurrying back and forth from the fort meant: Mr. Knipp and his men were leaving. There was no doubt at all in his mind that Father Bernard planned to stay behind. He was a decent white man, not the kind to run away like the agent. Any moment the bar on the door would slide back and the little man would enter, his sunburnt skull seeming to carry light and heat upon it.

A sudden shriek broke into his meditations. It was Jake Moon.

"A boat! A boat out there!"

"So, there is a boat."

"They're loading it, I see people hauling things aboard!"

His screeching annoyed Good Plume. "Be quiet," he said. "You'll wake the fat one. She will want to see too."

"What's going on?" whispered Jake.

"They are emptying the fort, sneaking off like thieves," he answered, hearing a noise from a far part of the room. That would be Red Blanket, he thought, wanting water and food. He wondered where the priest was.

Jake was hopping in his excitement. "Now the father can let us out!" He shouted out the window. "Hurry up! Open the door!" and turned to Good Plume, his eyes shining. "I never wanted to be in here, but that Mr. Knipp, he made me, and as soon as I get where I can do it I intend to lodge a complaint against him, just watch me!"

He would let no one else near the window, aroused and eager for his freedom, watching the path for the priest. Good Plume left him to it while he tended to No Leg, who complained loudly all during his inept ministrations, asking for the no-scalp man. It upset the others who also began to fret about his prolonged absence. In disgust Good Plume went back to the place against the wall worn shiny from his continued usage, the rough dirt of the floor smoothed to fit his buttocks.

Jake Moon was hanging onto the bars, his fingers white with strain, a light moaning coming from his throat.

"What is it?" the Indian asked in rising fear.

"He is leaving with them," Jake said. "I saw his black skirts and his black hat go on board." And he reached the door first, his hands pushing it, then beating on it with his fists, sobbing.

Good Plume's weight helped not at all. Red and panting, tears tracking his face, Jake at last gave it a name. "Betrayed," he said and slumped to the floor.

Later he went and hid under the thin blanket on his bed. Good Plume heard his cries, a thin mewing. "Oh my good Jesus, oh my good Jesus." Stoically the Indian rested his head against the familiar wall and closed his eyes.

At sunset Jake quit his bed.

Bear's Head was mocking Red Blanket and Jake did not understand the language, but they seemed to be quarreling about some article of clothing. Bear's Head crawled off to a corner and sat there, sulking, the winner flourishing from his bed a piece of blue cloth, taunting him. At a sharp command from Good Plume the winner put it away.

"Damned beggars," said Good Plume. "How many are there of them in here?"

Jake had recovered his voice, if not his nerve. "I think there are nine." He scratched at a sore on his arm that had not wanted to heal like the others and began to curse, monotonously and fervently, then stuck his fingers in his mouth and bit meanly, drawing blood. Maybe he could bleed to death instead of dying of hunger.

"Why do you swear like that? It's tiresome to listen to, besides having no variety. Now. Are there nine Indians or is there a crooked white man among us I haven't yet seen?"

"Nine Indians," Jake answered and chewed at another knuckle. "Seven men, three squaws," came from around it.

"Any dead, or dying, or apt to die?"

"Who knows?" Jake said. "Who goes around feeling of them? They're not my business."

"Oh but they are. Of this moment. It was your people who put us in here and ran away, leaving us imprisoned. That makes you responsible for us."

"Not me!" Enraged, Jake jumped up and down. He yelled, "Damn it, it's not my job to see to sick people, or dead ones either!"

Good Plume caught at his hand. He studied the bleeding fingers and spoke to them. "I can cut off one of you for each minute he wastes." He had no knife, but Jake did not stop to reason that out.

He rushed to the nearest bunk. Leaning down he whispered to Poor Elk. "Sit up, you bastard, sit up so the chief can see you're not dead." He shoved him to a sitting position. "See this one?" he yelled. "He's fine!" The last of the light shone wickedly from Poor Elk's eyes and he dropped him in haste. He shoved a woman from her blanket and propped her against a post. "Don't lean on me, you whore," he hissed. Her face was pitted with red sores where she had picked away the scabs; her eyes rolled wildly and she slid to the ground when he released her.

"She smiles pretty as a flower," he hollered to Good Plume, and kicked her in the ribs, careful not to be seen.

He did not stop until all were accounted for. Then Good Plume lost interest and rummaged among the priest's few belongings until he found the flint. He lit his pipe, grunting at Jake as he drew on the stem.

Jake pulled his hat down over his face and let pity for himself thin his blood.

On the far side of his mind Good Plume felt a small prick of sympathy for the youth hiding from the future behind a piece of dirty felt. Jake was too gentle in nature to handle what lay before them, but he was white, and that made him valuable to the others who had left on the boat. Good Plume believed it was only a matter of time before they would send someone to retrieve him, that in some manner they would contrive to rescue him, freeing Good Plume too.

So, it would be to his advantage to save the youth from despairing too deeply, and thought of rescue spurred him to act.

He got to his feet. "It stinks like hell in here," he announced, pinching his nose with his thumb and forefinger. "Why is it?"

"It's the hole, the pit over in the corner. I suppose it is full," Jake said from under his hat.

"We stink, too. Everything is foul, dirty, our clothing and blankets. Let's bury them," Good Plume suggested. "We can go without, the weather is warm enough."

"I am not digging any holes for any Indians," said Jake.

"I will help."

"It's too dark."

"I have the priest's flint. We can light a candle." There was no oil left for the lamp, but a box of candles sat on the bench where the water bucket was kept.

Jake pushed his hat up onto his forehead. He hadn't much liked the smothering feeling it gave him anyway. He stared at Good Plume's grinning face, the man who had been threatening to cut off his fingers a few moments ago. "Oh, well, if you want," he said.

They lit a candle. The Tooth sat on the edge of her bed, watching, her eyes fiery in its feeble light. Good Plume handed her the box of candles to care for, to keep mice from eating them, and as soon as the men moved away she nibbled at one since she had had nothing to eat. The wax stuck to her teeth and the taste was unpleasant; she decided if mice liked to eat them she could use them for bait. When she had caught enough of the creatures, then she could feast on them. She scratched her sores and licked her lips in anticipation.

The small shovel with the broken handle stood in the corner. Jake picked it up.

"I don't think I can do it," he told the old man as they drew near the odorous pit.

"Once, when I was a boy," Good Plume said, holding the candle high while Jake began to dig, "I was with my mother at a camp far off to the east where some Frenchmen lived by a big lake, and one of them gave me a piece of what was called cake, and when I went to eat it I saw it full of little brown droppings. I thought they were deer shit and was most amazed to think white men ate such things, but the man told me they were raisins. Fruit. Dried grapes, he said, and my mother acknowledged it was true. I ate the cake. It was the most delicious thing I have ever put in my mouth. I can remember even now how those raisins tasted, so sweet on my tongue. I have never had raisins since them, even though Mr. Knipp had them in his store."

Jake stopped to wipe the sweat from his face. "Why didn't you buy some from him?"

"The memory of them on my tongue I felt would be better than the actual taste—when one is old it all changes, I did not want that. I have noticed even water is never so sweet or cold as when I was a child. I think it would be the same with raisins."

"I wish you wouldn't talk of food or water."

The new pit was almost deep enough and the candle was danger-ously short. Jake had used the new dirt to cover the old latrine, and after much loud arguing Good Plume managed to get the blankets and some clothing from the Indians, using a stick to carry them to the shallow hole.

"They won't give up all their clothes," he told Jake. "They think the priest will come back and be angry to find them naked."

"He won't be back," Jake said flatly.

"Maybe not the father, but somebody will come. Your people won't abandon you, no more than mine would me, if any were alive."

Jake lay on his bed, waiting for moonrise. He wondered if what Good Plume had said was possible, that Mr. Knipp or Father Bernard would send someone back for him, then thought bitterly the old man was wrong; he didn't know the white man's heart at all. He cursed softly under his breath, slowly becoming aware of his words and listened to them curi-ously and had to admit his swearing was monotonous, as the old Indian had claimed, and he vowed to enlarge his vocabulary when he got to civilization.

⌒

GRASS HEART UNKNOWINGLY TOOK THE SAME PATH as her father's and came out from the woods into the pasture south of the fort. There she found only an old mule who had broken through a fence and was busily engaged in eating the last of the green grass under the trees, and who ran away from her when she approached it, in a bent-legged gait that re-minded her of her father.

The fort was empty of life, filled with ghosts, and she walked warily among them. A few books, some old clothing, and broken articles were strewn about. In what had been the kitchen bits of china lay on the floor. Everywhere there were rats, big sleek creatures who watched her with-out fear. Mr. Knipp had hated rats; he had them poisoned, trapped, or shot, and went so far as to import cats from downriver who promptly went wild. If nothing else was more proof of the total evacuation of the fort, the rats were enough, and she went out into the square where the wind blew dust across the yard, scrap paper swept up into it flying aimlessly aloft.

She found the ladder leading to the guard-walk and ascended, resting her arms on the parapet and staring out over the river.

How long ago had it been when the strange boat had taken away the white men? She rubbed her eyes. The wind blew harder, and storm clouds came sliding up the sky, black and purple, lightning shafts among them, but she did not move. There was nowhere to go.

⤺

BENEATH THE SLOTTED WINDOW, Good Plume lay on the dirt floor, his eyes fixed on a sky fattening with the promise of rain. A hard wind blew clots of clouds across his narrowed vision and he waited eagerly for the first drops of moisture to fall.

Jake had rigged up a water-catcher. He had broken a narrow piece from a bed slat and tied the handle of the pail to its end, battering it with his shovel head to flatten the vessel so that it would fit through the bars. In it they caught what rain that fell, and from the rags tied to the stick, which the morning dews dampened, they squeezed out the scarce liquid, then sucked on the wrung-out rags. What they garnered had been given to wet the mouths of the sick ones in the hut.

Poor Elk had awakened them one morning with shouts, and as they scrambled to her side they caught a glimpse of the rat disappearing through the window. That night no one slept; all were armed with pieces of wood from the bunks, and they killed two large rats, their fur bloody, their bodies sleek. Jake refused to eat them, but soon put aside his revulsion and gnawed on the uncooked bones without caring. The rats continued to come and the people ate them, The Tooth still preferring mice for their tenderness.

Now the pail clattered in the wind, and Good Plume watched the clouds, sucking on the little stone he kept in his mouth against the thirst that consumed him. He had ceased to hope for release from their prison. He regretted many things, but at that moment, most bitterly, the loss of the shovel. He and Jake Moon had attempted to dig a tunnel with it. The ground had been hard, the shovel head dull, and the handle, already broken, had finally shattered, leaving them staring at the small hole, barely opened. He had fallen into a rage, frightening Jake, who tried to dig again with it by pushing the blade with his hands. It had been a useless effort, and from sheer weakness he had fallen over onto the dirty blade, cutting his cheek. It did not heal well; a jagged wound whose edges leaked green pus, and Good Plume spied on it, losing heart. The young man sat hunched against the hated door, his head propped on his arms. Bugs crawled along his hairline and he did not brush them away.

"How long have we been here?" Good Plume asked the indifferent figure, wanting to touch him, to comfort him, but not daring to.

"I don't know," Jake mumbled. "I'd guess some weeks." Then he raised his eyes and looked at Good Plume. "Are you all right, chief?" he said. In spite of the cracked voice he sounded alarmed.

"I'm all right. But I can't remember how water tastes, or how it feels to swallow it, all I want of it. Here we are with the river just outside the door, so close, and we can't reach it. I listen to it and hear it talking to me. It asks me why I don't come to it, why I stay away." He glanced down at his feet, somewhat embarrassed. "We're old friends, that river and me. We've been living next to each other since I was born. I know it like a brother." He paused and watched the pail swing in the wind for a while. "I guess when I no longer hear it talking to me I will know I am dying."

"It's sure to rain, then you can drink all we catch this time. I'm not that thirsty anymore."

The old man continued, as though Jake had not spoken, a far-off look lighting his face. "I always believed I would die in battle—that was when I was young and gave good account of myself in fighting. Then in my middle years I began to think less of that and looked forward to a peaceful death in my lodge, everybody sad at my going, my daughter especially so. I would be an old man, honored and wise, and my spirit would be content to leave my body to join my ancestors, far to the north where the sky ends. There are no troubles there; no sickness, no eyes that can't see, no bad legs or cut-off arms. Everybody is young, or at least at that age they most want to be, and there is food, whatever you like best to eat, and nobody is ever too cold or too hot, and the fires never go out.

"So. I am old, but in prison. My spirit can't escape from a prison. I will die here and it will count for nothing."

Many Buffalo left off picking at her sores and listened to the old man talking to the white man. These were the only things that kept her occupied during the long days—the talking and the picking at the sores. She had lost all interest in anything else. All of her earlier pleasures seemed to have occurred to someone else altogether: the handsome men; the presents they gave her when she lay with them; the whiskey she sometimes stole while they slept; the dances, wild and joyful, with their drums leading her feet around, her knees bending, her thighs shivering until her back arched and she felt weak with abandonment and fell to the earth.

Many Buffalo wished the two men would argue and get angry as they used to do; it was exciting then and gave her a feeling of life, after being dead so long. This day they talked too low for her to hear them well. And the white man seemed to fear he would fall asleep, for he started to slap himself and pinch his ears, and pace about the room. He came close to where she lay, stopped and stared at her, his face ugly with its seeping wound, the pock marks like red paint. He was thin, too, so thin that his blue eyes stuck out from their sockets. She tried to envision what he had looked like before coming to this place, with fat on his bones and smiling at everyone.

She knew he was troubled by what the old man had said about dying; that much she had caught with her sharp ears. Maybe the white man feared death too. She guessed he was mostly frightened that the old Indian would die first and leave him alone. The rest of the people in the pesthouse did not matter to him, she knew; most wouldn't last long without water and better food than a few rats and mice, and would die anyway. Her dull mind refused to dwell on it any longer and she went back to picking at her sores, dimly conscious that he had gone over to Good Plume and was shaking him.

"Wake up! Don't give up!" he shouted, but his throat pained and his voice failed him. He wanted desperately to cry. He lacked even tears.

"Go away," said Good Plume pleasantly. "I am preparing to sing."

↩

GRASS HEART STOOD ON THE GUARD-WALK. The wind pushed the river against the shore, small waves breaking and falling away. She let her gaze rest on them, until the rim of her eye caught a movement, less rhythmic, frantic, beyond an elm tree at the northern edge of the riverbank. There something flapped in the wind, fastened to a stick.

She climbed down the ladder and ran out the gates, finding a weed-grown path that led to a low building set back in the trees. The wood it was made of was weathered to a gray the same shade as the sky, and as she drew near she saw cloths snapping from the stick, their colors faded and soiled. They beckoned to her.

Bending down she peered within the narrow slit they signaled. There was nothing there but darkness and silence.

Poor Elk was the first to see the face at the window. She did not truly believe it was there. She screamed anyway.

At the sound the heavy bar fell from the door. It flew open. A strange girl, howling and crying, threw herself within and onto the old Indian. They wept together.

Poor Elk screamed again when the girl attacked the white man and whirled him madly about.

Jake Moon fainted. Good Plume laughed and pounded the fallen man on his back, waking him up. Then the three of them lay in a heap on the ground and laughed even more.

Poor Elk knew not what to make of it and crept from her bed to look. She clutched her only piece of clothing around her waist and stood next to them, giggling at their behavior.

Grass Heart found herself facing a pair of bare legs. Enough light from the window fell on them and she swallowed convulsively.

"*Maggots,*" she whispered, then yelled: "Great bloody Jesus!" Throwing the door open as wide as it would go she swept through the room, raging and cursing. She seized her stick from where it had dropped from her hand and began to beat Jake Moon with it. The Tooth had been wormy for so long she had grown accustomed to them, noticing them first on her stomach, wriggling in the sores that lingered there, and she wondered why the girl was so upset. Worms weren't that bad.

They helped one another outside, where a light rain fell, and they threw back their heads in delight, their parched bodies drinking in the moisture.

Grass Heart made them show her their sores. They looked curiously as she inspected them, Many Buffalo finding a huge hole in one breast she had not noticed before, where the maggots squirmed, fat and sluggish, easy to remove.

An old man was the worst afflicted; he was rolled onto his belly; his buttocks were full of holes and nests of worms wriggled there. The Tooth dug them out and dropped them to earth while the old man moaned and gurgled and heaved himself about.

"They ate better than we did," said Many Buffalo as she stomped happily on them with her dirty feet. And when they looked into his face to find it half eaten away, Grass Heart said, "I'd rather look at his ass, anytime."

It made Jake Moon blush, and he ran as well as he could to the river, hopping on one foot and then the other to remove his worn-out boots, to float there, his toes to the sky. Good Plume was already there, lying in the shallows, his mouth open in song. Jake observed him most tenderly, and Grass Heart, seated cross-legged on the bank, watched him with an intensity that burned her eyes.

The clouds cleared off, the sun came out, bright and cheerful. Green flies and gnats brought the swimmers from the water, and Jake and Grass Heart went off to the kitchen gardens of the fort where they dug about, fetching back a few good squash and overripe ears of corn. Good Plume brought wood, and with the flint made a fire. In their rags the Indians lay or sat, talking quietly, taking sparing sips from the pail of water that No Leg brought. Each one had bathed in the cool river, all but the old man with the rotten face and buttocks, who lay apart from the rest, for he smelled of putrefaction so strongly that the others shunned him.

Then the moon showed in the east, the little one they called the buffalo calf moon because of its horns, and all were exhausted and fell asleep in the nests they hollowed out in the overgrown grass with leafy branches to cover them.

A triumphant Grass Heart watched over all.

⤺

THE TOOTH AND THE OLD MAN stayed behind, waiting until he was fit to travel, while the rest of the Indians from the pesthouse left for the upriver villages, avoiding the one across the river.

Good Plume crossed alone to it after retrieving Grass Heart's bullboat from below the fort. He found but a few survivors. The village had been cleared of the dead, those who could be identified placed in the forks of trees in the deep woods. The unknown, mainly skeletons and scattered bones, were put into a pit dug into the hillside below the gardens. He learned the Sioux had raided the village shortly after Grass Heart had set out on her search and had stolen the horses and plundered the gardens, carrying off the harvest.

He returned with a black heart, his face ferocious, and Jake Moon went cautiously away from him into the fort where he had a room he had outfitted with odds and ends and where he slept. He found The Tooth there. She had washed her hair with the soapy liquid from the yellow cactus and was combing it with a bent fork she had found. It shone blackly.

She felt his eyes on her and drew the tines more gently through her long hair, her head drooping, her eyes cast sideways toward his. A slow smile lifted her lips.

"Where's the old uncle?" he asked. His hands were nervous and he tried to put them in his pockets without success.

"He went home," she said.

"Thought you were going too."

There was a significance in the look she gave him that caused his stomach to tighten.

"Nothing there for me and nobody waiting." She rose and came to where he was perched on a wooden box and kissed him full on the lips. It was quite a professional kiss, practiced and full of promise, and he clasped her about the waist and dropped her to the floor.

It took no time at all. Jake was stunned, and remained there, his mouth open and his eyes shut. The Tooth rose, shook out her hair, and shuffled off to the river to wash it again.

Neither Good Plume nor Grass Heart were surprised when The Tooth made her bed on the floor next to Jake's and fell without protest into the tasks of fetching water and wood and cooking the few provisions they found in the pit beneath the kitchen that had not been ravaged by the rats and mice.

Jake delayed his plans for leaving. Not because of The Tooth, although he admitted to himself he was unlikely to ever experience again such a variety and degree of sexual excitement as she gave him so willingly, but rather that he felt bound somehow to Good Plume. And his concern and affection for the old man demanded that he see to his safety, so he stayed.

When Jake proposed that they move to the village, Grass Heart argued against it, saying they were safer where they were, that there was plenty of wood, shelter, and game nearby in the timber. Good Plume said he didn't care. It was as good a place as any, and that the village was filled with ghosts.

"The Sioux are sure to come here," warned The Tooth, "they ain't about to pass up the chance anything was left."

She proved surprisingly adept at picking out hiding places for each of them, and Jake wondered where she had learned such skill but had a feeling it would not be wise to ask. And one day, when Grass Heart was on watch, the Sioux came, a band of gaily painted warriors appearing on the rimrock above the fort. She slipped away to warn the others.

They came down into the pastures and left their horses there, and crept along the fence to the walls. The main body entered by the yawning gates and walked boldly about, laughing and shouting.

Grass Heart and The Tooth lay concealed in the kitchen pit, dirt sprinkled over its small wooden door by Jake before he ran through the porches to hide in the hollowed-out hay bales stacked against the stable wall. Good Plume was already there, and they faced each other, blinking the dust from their eyes and praying they would not sneeze. Crouched there, the old Indian holding the short spear, Jake with empty hands, they listened intently.

The raiders did not enter the stable, and they walked across the dirt floor of the kitchen without examining anything but the cupboards. It was a careless, cursory search; they found nothing of any value to them and left as they came, but not before trying to set the store on fire. It would not burn satisfactorily. They gave up, leaving behind them a few charred timbers and a great deal of smoke.

"If they'd been serious about it they would have found us," Jake said thoughtfully.

They had gathered together in the stable. It was dusky and smelled of must.

The Tooth grinned and patted him on the shoulder, saying, "They was serious enough, they just are stupid peoples. Stupid shit-peoples," she added.

"Bloody goddamn stupid shit-peoples," said Grass Heart.

Good Plume looked at her with disapproval but said nothing; he would never have the heart to scold her ever again. Jake coughed, feeling his face flush.

"It's their women who are the smart ones," The Tooth remarked, and waited. No one said anything, but Grass Heart winked at her.

"I've dirt in my hair," The Tooth said after a while, and went off to the river, feeling cross.

She did not return that night, and when they searched for her at first light they found no sign of her anywhere.

The bent fork she used as a comb was gone from its place when Jake remembered to look for it. He said nothing about it to the others, but he was morose and seldom spoke for days afterwards.

⌐

GRASS HEART FINALLY AGREED to accompany Jake and her father to the village. The survivors had left for the winter village, a pitiful few walking, their possessions tied atop camp dogs.

The two men prowled through the lodges for things they would need for the winter. Jake did not hesitate to enter the empty lodges; he looked for tools and weapons and clothing, finding more than he expected, for the people had disturbed nothing of the dead after removing the bodies, just drawing the deer hide curtains, shutting in the spirits remaining there.

A cold wind whistled through the streets, a sad, empty song that throbbed in Grass Heart's head so that she did not linger long, but gathered what she needed and waited for the others on the riverbank.

Time passed quickly in the fort. The first snow fell; the geese and ducks and swans rode the wind south, and in the mornings a light crust of ice edged the water, the sun lower in the sky when she did appear. The three of them had meat to eat after Good Plume fashioned new arrows for the bows they brought from the village.

At first, Jake Moon saw little game because of his lack of skill in hunting. He ploughed through the woods, dead leaves crunching underfoot and branches breaking with loud cracks when he passed through thickets. In time he learned how to stalk the game that had moved in after the white men had left the fort and that fed in the open pastures. In the beginning, Good Plume went with him on those days when the air was mild;

otherwise he remained next to the stove in the kitchen where Grass Heart worked and nursed his aching knee.

There had been a touching reunion between Jake and Posey. He insisted on bringing her into a room to winter, fearful she might be stolen by some passing Indian, and there he fed her on armloads of hay he brought from the stables and stacks along the fences. She grew fat again and seemed to thrive with his attention.

She was the only remaining thing that reminded Jake that he was still white. His appearance had altered remarkably, and he first noticed it one day while sitting on a high bluff, waiting for deer to come down to drink from the creek.

He wore a shaggy buffalo robe about his upper body, with leggins beneath it. On his feet were elkskin boots. His beloved hat had long ago been lost, and his head was covered with a hood of wolf fur the color of old snow. He hurried to the creek and, bending over, looked with slow astonishment into a small, clear pool. The icy winds and sun on the snow had darkened his skin to a deep brown. Only his blue eyes, a startling color against his dusky flesh, saved him from being taken for an Indian.

He could not see the colors in the water but he knew they were there.

Safe in Posey's room, he hugged her. She raised her flat ugly head and blew a round bubble from her nose. A shaft of sunlight from a crack shone on it. A rainbow grew there. He poked with a tentative finger at it until it burst, then laid his head against her neck and wept for all the cruelties in the world.

As winter lingered, the mule grew irritable from her long confinement and, unnoticed, took to eating the empty wooden boxes along one wall. She chewed on shelves and nibbled pieces from a heavy bench in a corner. When Jake raked out the manure she dropped, he did it hurriedly and missed seeing the bits of wood in it.

She began to lose weight, so lean her bones were but a rack the skin hung from, and Jake took her outside, clearing the snow away from the brown brittle grass, hoping a change in diet would improve her health. She continued to decline, and he found her stiff in death one dreary morning.

Grass Heart, shocked at his display of bereavement, took her butcher knife and cut through the mule's neck and showed him the throat laddered with wooden splinters. They had prevented her from eating. Jake went off into the woods to grieve, blaming himself for her death. He was a long time recovering from his loss.

As for Grass Heart, she labored at cleaning the game Jake brought back, cursing herself when she cut her hands while skinning or burned them as she cooked food, her hair untended and her clothing grimed from smoke and blood. At night she suffered terrible nightmares; in her dreams she relived the evils of the summer, and struggled in her sleep.

Good Plume never fully regained his strength, although his sleep was untroubled. He was prone to keep to his bed most days, where he lay propped up, smoking his pipe, his thoughts vaguely drifting; he had no anchor to hold them with, no future to which he could fasten them.

His wants were few and he asked for less. Sometimes he was struck with the idea his heart had died; he would press his hands against his breast and frantically feel for its beating, only to find its steady thrust against his ribs, reassuring him until the next time it came into his mind that death was reaching for him.

⌐

THEY AWOKE ONE MORNING TO FIND the wind, tired of the snow plains, coming out of the south, bearing vast flocks of birds whose wings filled the air with thunder. The three of them climbed the rotting boards of the parapet to watch their flight and feasted on their flesh that night. In the darkness before sleep Good Plume heard their voices filling the valley as they fled northward, knowing new leaves would soon green along the river, the sun lifting blades of new grass from the earth, while snow drifts died under its touch.

With the new warmth, water ran everywhere: down the folds of the hills, into the river, and the ice rose up, rotted slabs clashing and battering, and like great rafts they sailed downriver bearing huge trees and herds of buffalo and elk caught when their trenched trails across the ice beds fell into the swift flowing waters, their bellows lost in the thunder of the flood.

Each day Grass Heart mounted to the guard-walk and searched the opposite bank of the river, rewarded at last by the sight of plumes of smoke rising above the roofs of the village. She helped her father climb the ladder, and they counted the blue and scarlet cloths that appeared on long poles over each dwelling, so few of them that she grew thoughtful and took him down into the fort again. When the river dropped enough so they could cross safely, and before the snow melt from the far-off mountains caused new flooding, Jake and Grass Heart, with newly made paddles, rowed her father across. He lay back, one blue-veined hand slicing through the dark, swiftly moving water.

An old woman at the gate sighted them and called the others. People came running down the path to the shore, calling to them as they came near. The greetings were subdued, muffled sobs coming from some of the women, the men grunting as they searched the faces of Good Plume and his daughter. Jake was subjected to a cold, hard-eyed scrutiny, with murmurs of hostility coming from the crowd. He met it unflinchingly, and Good Plume put his arms around his shoulders, indicating his affection for him to the people who had good reason to despise all white men.

The women clicked their tongues at Grass Heart; she self-consciously fingered her lank braids. But her face was sharp, with angles and planes foreign to it, yet proud: it hid her shame well.

No one followed them to their old lodge. The door lay back along the porch entrance, the latch and hinges twisted and broken by apparent hatchet blows. Indoors, the scene that met them was so bleak that gloom settled over Grass Heart.

Without a word she set to work, separating the broken pots and dusty robes. Jake Moon brought water and wood. Good Plume found his shield, too large to take last winter when they had been there, smashed beyond repair, and held his hand over his breast, feeling for his heart once again.

Soon a fire was made, a blackened kettle scrubbed out with sand set to boil, meat they had brought with them filling the room with the good smell of stewing ribs. As they ate, their talk was desultory, innocent; no one spoke of the past, and little was said of the future.

Not too long after they were settled some elderly men came to the lodge to discuss Jake Moon's presence in the village.

"We want him driven away," an elder said, refusing the pipe that Good Plume had lit and was passing among them. They were sitting outdoors, on willow backrests that Grass Heart had repaired with new withes, a gentle breeze stirring the new leaves and the gray hairs on their heads. "We want him sent away now," he continued. "He was one of those who brought the sickness here."

Good Plume had hoped there would be no protest made against Jake's living among them and set his jaw like an angry badger. He regarded the speaker Elk Walking, a former friend, with distaste.

"There is no reason for him to leave. He is a guest in my lodge. Even if he wished to, I could not allow it; the Sioux are between him and the forts below."

"We are all in agreement he must go," Elk Walking retorted.

"If I do anything with my good friend Jake Moon it will be to marry him to my daughter. Then he would be one of my family. I wouldn't mind that. He is a good hunter, and brave, and would care for me in my last days," said Good Plume, casting a meaningful glance toward the speaker.

Elk Walking had wed his daughter to a French trapper who beat her readily, and who lost a leg in an accident, and had moved in with her family, and many times Elk Walking had complained to Good Plume what a burden they were on him.

There was little more to be said, so far as Good Plume was concerned, and there seemed to be a tacit agreement among the elders that nothing further would change conditions, and they went away.

When Jake Moon learned of the discussion he was amused at Good Plume's cunning. Grass Heart told him to pay no attention to any unfriendly acts on the part of the old men. "If it wasn't for those eyes of yours you'd look like a damned Indian like the rest of us. And I don't intend to marry any white man, especially you. They can throw you to the Sioux first," she said and laughed merrily.

He felt chagrin and relief both, wanting only to leave that poor, falling-down village with its vacant, echoing lodges. Looking about him he thought wryly how he had attained his youthful desire to live like an Indian, and after the pesthouse he also knew how it was to die as one, and he shuddered at the remembrance.

Summer came, and there was the planting of gardens to be completed, the hoarded seeds brought forth and put in the ground. And there were buffalo hunts; without horses to ride and to pack the meat on, the able-bodied men and women walked with anticipation out across the prairies, lance in hand, bow strung from a shoulder, all working together after the kill to strip the hides and carry the great bloody chunks of meat back to the village. There it was cut into strips and dried on small scaffolds in the sun, the humps and tongues eaten with relish in the green twilight.

The village resounded to the scrape of bone instruments on the hides stretched out on pegs before the lodges. And sometimes in the evenings there were other sounds, those of play, when the few young people gathered at the old dancing ground and persuaded an old man to bring out his drum. They danced, but it was never really the same, and eventually they discontinued that pleasure. What courting was done was carried out under the avid eyes of the elders, the gifts meager and the ceremony done quickly, and a pregnant woman was an object revered by the entire village, since there were but thirty-one families left of the Mandan.

Grass Heart waited for the free traders to come, bringing salt, sugar, coffee, and the iron bars to melt down for shot, and powder for the few guns in the village. She was ready to barter the furs of fox and wolf and marten that Jake had learned to trap, but the little pirogues never came, only the steamboats hurrying upriver to Fort Union.

At first some of the curious went to the shore to watch them, but by late summer just Jake Moon and Good Plume stood on the riverbank, and then not often, one looking wistfully at the boats, the other grim-faced.

⤴

IN LATE SUMMER SWEET FLAG rode into the village on a dainty white and yellow mare, brass rosettes braided into its mane and a crown of raven feathers across its brow. Sweet Flag wore a simple gown, but bore on his arms many bracelets of copper and iron, his earrings of the finest silver work. The whip that dangled from his wrist was a white swan's wing. The mare danced sideways along the street, and the rider bowed and smiled as he made his way to his old lodge at the edge of the town.

Grass Heart was the first to visit him. "I thought you were dead," she said, and embraced him.

He wriggled from her arms and told her, "Not I! I escaped!" and he preened as he undid his long sleek braids. "I left the first day, after Seven Birds' mother fell sick. A friend and I went to the Minneconjou camp, west on Old Woman Creek, and have traveled with them since then. We went on to the mountains to the west and they had a big fight there with the Crow, and after that other things happened," his voice falling away.

He fondled his earrings and laid them on a fur robe. "I liked seeing all the places I went but don't like fighting, and the Minneconjou fight often.

"I am tired, you must forgive me," and he ushered her to the door politely.

She bathed in the river, washing her hair and greasing it till it shone. She dug out her one good gown, her best moccasins, first rubbing sweet grass on her limbs and body. Clad in a red blanket she sped out the door, Good Plume's bewildered face turning to watch.

She knocked on Sweet Flag's doorpost and entered before he could call out. He was seated by the fire, quilling a neckband, and looked up in alarm. "What do you want here?" He pricked his finger with the awl; blood ran from it.

"Here," she said and went to him, taking the band of doeskin from him. "Blood is very hard to clean off, you know."

He sucked at his finger, his plucked eyebrows raised.

"I have such trouble keeping my dresses soft—and clean, well, you know how dirty one gets making fires, and *cooking!* Oh God I hate to cook!"

She stole a look at him.

He continued. "Once I tried animal brains on my gowns, the Minneconjou use that method, but I couldn't *bear* the smell."

"Use white clay," Grass Heart said, deftly wielding the awl and thinking how strange the conversation was, how peculiar they would look to anyone who came to the door.

She snapped the thread with her large white teeth and held the band out before her, giving it a critical eye. "The black is crooked, and there are gaps between the red and white quills," she said.

He said nothing, and she continued. "Any little girl not yet wearing moss between her legs could do a better job than this."

Quietly he said, "It's not very good, is it."

Something led her to look at him. His head drooped, suddenly, and he held his hands out and stared at them. Dirt was ingrained in the palms; the nails were shapely but torn and red skin rode their edges.

Then she noticed the lines in his face beneath the love circles of red paint on his cheeks and between his brows. His eyes were weary; shadows filled their corners. "Horse Catcher was wrong," he said. "I live a miserable life."

"I am sorry," she said.

"Yes. Well, perhaps it will end soon." And he smiled at her, the old, gentle way of their youth.

She ran home in tears.

⤚

JAKE MOON WAS HUNTING on foot when he found a horse.

In a coulee under a cutbank, where sometime before he had spied a den of foxes, he came upon a small, fat pony, bay colored, wearing a rope bridle. The single rein was sawn through and dangled just below her nose. She let him approach her with little more than a gentle snort and a half-hearted shying away, and when he caught her up she smelled of him with her muzzle, like a child with a flower. And when he went to mount her she stood very still.

She was a child's pony, he decided, and he put her at a walk, choosing the easiest way back to the village. Leading her proudly into the lodge he spread fresh grass in the pen and put her into it, then leaned against the railing in admiration.

He named her Idabelle, after his mother, and kept her hidden for a week, then ventured out after deer aboard her, mounted on a new saddle Grass Heart made him of elk skin stuffed with hay. Good Plume gave the animal a thorough examination, then pronounced her healthy. "Don't ride her hard, though," he warned, "until she's lost most of that fat."

Jake rode Idabelle whenever he went hunting after that, and she did lose weight, gradually, but he could never force her into a gallop; she trotted, a bone-wracking trot, stiff-legged and regal, and when he whipped her she stopped short, her neck rigid, and rolled her eyes in dismay.

Ashamed to have punished her so, he let her make her own stride, enduring it stoically. At last he gave over riding her at all, and she spent her days carrying children about the village and rolling in the dirt outside the gates, edging her way into the remnants of the horse herd, until Jake gave her up entirely, telling himself, bitterly, that she was as fickle and ungrateful as all the other females in his life, then hastily amended it to exclude Grass Heart, having forgotten the faithful Willow Woman and Mrs. Rosen altogether.

Summer left slowly. She gave the people a good harvest: great numbers of orange squash, pale yellow pumpkins, and ears of corn, plump kerneled, to gather and dry in the sun for winter eating.

On the day the Sioux came, Grass Heart was with the other women under an arbor sorting corn ears when the old woman who was guarding them began screeching and pointing to the west where, against the skyline, the riders appeared. The women scattered to their lodges, and Grass Heart from her porch looked back and saw them wind slowly down the slopes toward the garden, naked and unpainted and leading packhorses. Their voices were shrill on the clear, hot air as they stuffed the harvest into huge skin sacks and laid them over the animals' backs.

"I don't know why they bother to raid our gardens," Good Plume said aggrievedly when she told him. "We don't grow enough anymore to feed ourselves, let alone them." All that labor for nothing, he thought.

"You hide," he told her. "You and Poor Crow and the others." He thought the old ones would be safe, but not the four young women.

"I don't want to go without you," Grass Heart said. "They'll come here."

His snort was testy. "I don't feel like running off. At least hide yourself." He laid his white braids properly on his chest, saying, "A warrior does not hide nor run away."

She agreed to get under the pile of buffalo robes at the back of the lodge. They smelled, and it was hot beneath them, and she could not breathe, and slid out from under them in time to see Jake Moon dash through the door.

"You go now," Good Plume told him. "They hate white men. If they find you here they'll kill you."

"I don't think you should hang around."

"Us they only rob from, but you they would kill. Keep to the trees and go north along the river. Or there's time to swim to the other side."

"I never learned how. And the boats are gone. I saw the women leaving in them."

He shifted from one foot to the other and blinked his eyes; his indecision infuriated Grass Heart and she swore at him. "By Jesus you will go if I have to carry you on my back," she told him and punched him in the stomach.

"That won't be necessary," he said, rubbing where she had struck him.

"The door," she said suddenly. It had never been mended and still stood at the side of the lodge. "Help me carry it to the river."

Together they lifted it and took it down the path to the riverbank, where he threw himself aboard.

Grass Heart ran out into the shallows and pushed the door into the current. It whirled once, then righted itself and floated downstream, Jake flat on its surface, his chin full of slivers.

"Good-bye!" she called, but he was too busy to answer.

"Why didn't you go too?" Good Plume asked when she returned, and she gave him an indignant look and began to wring out her dress.

"I am tired of all these troubles," she said, and sat down in her wet gown and folded her hands in her lap.

She lifted them, peering at them, then opened them as though she were releasing something she no longer wanted, brushing them together, bemused; and Good Plume regarded her with love, smiling at the sight of his beautiful daughter. He picked up his lance and waited.

⌒

GOOD PLUME STUMBLED when the toe of his moccasin caught under the lip of a pine root. His captor jerked on the rope tied to his waist, saying, "I don't know why Horse Runner let you live. I've a mind to let you go, you've been nothing but trouble. But then I'd be hard punished, so better the whip on your back than on mine," and flicked the leather whip over the old man's shoulders; his teeth glistened as he laughed at the snap it made.

"See to it you don't mark me up," said Good Plume. "Horse Runner thinks of me as his brother and wouldn't like to see my blood."

The warrior stopped his horse and pulled on the rope. "Show me your scars again," he said. Good Plume obligingly raised the fringe of hair from his eyes, exposing the ugly pock marks.

"Aarrrgh," said the man, "revolting." He wiped his nose on a bit of red cloth and nudged his mount with his knee.

When they stopped again, Good Plume sank to the ground and rubbed his knee with his bound hands. He gazed out over the land. All of it was strange to him. It had been a long time since he had ridden out on the prairies beyond sight of the river, and he could not recognize this place, with its sere grass waving in the wind and a hint of low hills to the west. The sun was hidden now and clouds ran across the sky, streamers of gray tasting of rain.

"How did Horse Runner get the smallpox?" he asked, watching the clouds.

"He was a boy, and his mother took him with her to visit a trader's camp where they both fell sick. She died there, and they shoveled her in the earth. Horse Runner lived. On the day of her death he swore to avenge her, and I must say it has taken much white men's blood to satisfy him and he's not done yet. The rest of us like to fight the white men too, but sometimes we get tired of it. He don't. He wants to wipe them from the earth."

His captor wasn't a bad man, Good Plume thought. He treated him well, like this moment, and saw he had water and food enough to keep him on his feet. And the fellow liked to talk. It was to Good Plume's interest to let him.

"I've known a few white men," he continued, "who were pretty good men. No harm in them. Like one we found living with a band of Santee last winter far to the east of here. My eldest son was with me and took the coughing sickness. This white man treated him, but then Horse Runner rode in with a bad temper when he lost a fight with some soldiers. That was the end of *that* white man. He called himself a priest. A little man who died bravely."

"What happened to your son?" asked the old man.

"He got well." He gestured, and Good Plume reluctantly got to his feet. "We couldn't scalp that white man," the warrior said and scowled.

"He had no hair."

The prairie stretched huge and empty, but for the two lines of captives far ahead. He could not make out their numbers, nor where Grass Heart walked among them. A few drops of rain fell on his head, and he pulled at his blanket to cover it. He felt his heart lurch, frighteningly, and sadness overcame him, as gray and dismal as the rain that began to fall.

When Horse Runner had come into the lodge, he had been ready to die. But another man had snatched his spear from him before he could use it. He was readying himself to sing his death song but lost the chance when Horse Runner grasped his hair and drew back his head, knife ready. With an exclamation the warrior let it go, brushed back the hair fringe from his forehead, and knelt to see the pox marks beneath.

Smiling openly, he motioned the other warrior away and sat down next to Good Plume, who inspected him with caution.

Horse Runner was very tall, almost as tall as Good Plume, with thick arms and legs. His face was deeply pitted, and the pox scars dimpled his limbs. Speaking rapidly, he pointed to each one with a long dirty finger.

Good Plume knew enough of the Sioux language to follow what he said. Horse Runner told him the cursed white man's disease made them brothers, then picked at his teeth with a bear claw hanging about his neck. He seemed very pleased with his cruel, ugly face, touching it often.

His eyes were wide and woeful as he listened to the old man's account of his own scars, and the ordeal of the pesthouse, giving him over to Lost Weasel when he was finished.

Grass Heart remained silent all through this strange meeting and put up no resistance when the Sioux warrior with the scars took her by the hand and led her to an empty lodge, where he raped her, efficiently and politely, showing by his discreetness his respect toward her father. She was not greatly distressed, only a little sore; the man had not struck her nor torn her clothing, seeming to be acting more out of a duty than lust. Then she was hustled away and tied with the other captives by their hands to a long rope, and sent off without seeing her father again.

Horse Runner cautioned Lost Weasel to go slowly with the old man, as he was crippled. "He has already suffered enough. The white man not only gave him the sickness but they broke his leg too." He stressed emphatically that he be allowed to rest often, and embraced him when he left.

Good Plume asked for his good blanket, to take it with him, and Lost Weasel agreed to it. The old man was surprised; he had expected the fellow would refuse. He thought perhaps this imprisonment would not be as bad as the pesthouse, and resigned himself to it.

That night in Grass Heart's camp a warrior known as Dog Eater took her from the rope and hauled her into the trees. He was fat and smelled. Afterwards he gave her dried meat from his saddle bag and let her walk about, even allowing her to go to the creek in the grove to drink. And when she at last fell asleep, some other man pulled up her dress and she yelled, and bit the man in the leg. In the morning she was cross from lack of rest.

They reached the Sioux camp that afternoon, a large one set along a river in a fold of hills. She was surprised at the number of lodges, tall pointed dwellings made of hides, with crude paintings on their sides. Dog Eater led her to his and gave her to his wives, who promptly beat her and put her to work.

She grew thinner with each passing day, for sometimes they refused to feed her or else forgot. She worked like the slave she had become; she grew careless of her appearance, her hair uncombed, her dress stained and ragged. Her moccasins wore out and she went barefoot.

Dog Eater came for her one night and led her by a leather thong about her neck to the Captive's Dance. She heard the drums and dragged her feet, and almost fell when he pushed her into the circle.

The shrill chanting hurt her ears; the stones and sticks thrown at her raised welts on her body and made her angry. Children darted in to spit on the captives and she hissed at them, the white spot in her eye red in the firelight. The warriors circled about them, leaping and shouting, but the women remained in an outer circle, shuffling their feet in a curious heel and toe movement that she thought ungainly and amusing. Among her people the women danced like the men, graceful and proud.

Finally it was over, and Dog Eater handed her over to his youngest wife, who took her to the place where the spectators watched. Grass Heart could only wait patiently, her eyes averted from their grinning faces. She felt a sudden yearning for the rounded lodges of home, the river in its valley, the familiar smells and sounds of her village. She growled in her throat when the young wife yanked her by the neck impatiently and swore at her as they began walking back to the lodge.

Dodging a random stick, she heard her name called, and looking about she saw her father standing alone nearby. There was a look of wonderment on his face as she was pulled away.

He waited for her the next morning outside Dog Eater's lodge, wearing new moccasins and a brightly colored calico shirt. When she looked at him, his creased cheeks broke apart in a smile. "Holy Jesus," she said.

"You have a dirty face," he said accusingly. "And why are you so thin?"

Outraged, she stamped her feet rapidly and cried, "I am dirty because I am a slave! Slaves don't wear fine clothing, slaves don't get fed, slaves don't sleep on furs and oil their hair all day. Nobody gives a God damn for a slave!"

"I have looked all over for you," he said in astonishment. "I thought some warrior had made you his wife, hiding you away in his teepee." His chin was quivering.

"No one has wanted to marry me since you ran off to live in that pesthouse," she told him, then put her head into the cave of his shoulder and wept.

"Don't cry," he said, and patted her on the sharp bones of her back.

When the young wife Long Eye switched Grass Heart around her legs that afternoon, she slapped the woman across the face, a satisfyingly brutal blow that made the woman's nose spurt blood onto her gown. The wife fled into the lodge, and Grass Heart went off to the creek to bathe.

She scrubbed thoroughly with the white sand from the shore and lay in the stream, letting the water wash over her, cooling the fever that had risen in her blood. Small yellow finches flitted in and out of the branches that hung over the stream, and she pursed her lips and whistled the three notes of their song, slapping at the water with her calloused hands. She thought it was the happiest she had felt in a long time. She counted the ribs on her chest and promised herself to cover them with fat, and her hip bones too. She would be handsome again.

〜

GOOD PLUME AND HORSE RUNNER SMOKED together and discussed Grass Heart's situation.

"My only child should not be a slave," said Good Plume.

Horse Runner laid down his pipe and picked at his teeth with his bear claw, inspecting it thoughtfully when done. At last he said, "Slavery's not a bad thing in my opinion. We all do it to each other. Our mother the earth gave us animals and fruit to eat, wood to burn, and furs to keep us warm, and she put us here too, just as she did the buffalo and the trees and the rivers and lakes, and we use them as she planned, so it seems natural to use each other too." He paused, his forehead puzzled, and puffed at his pipe.

Good Plume was thinking it a rather weak argument, and when Horse Runner began a tirade about the white man's policy of plowing up the earth and planting fields of strange grasses to feed their animals instead of using what the mother earth had provided free for all on the prairies, he lost interest altogether.

He considered the Sioux a simple-minded people without much knowledge of the world, inclined to faulty reasoning. He thought that it was because they had no stability in life, moving about constantly as they did, making them as flighty and insubstantial as the wind. As for Horse Runner's censure of the white man's way of farming, Good Plume had seen it and knew how slavery had played an important part in it. He himself had never decided whether or not the use of slaves was a good thing or a bad one, and in a comparison of customs the Indian's ancient tradition of enslavement came out looking questionable.

He came out of his reverie to hear Horse Runner's statement that he would purchase Grass Heart from her owner. "Two ponies should be enough," he said. "I could throw in a few hands full of beads and some eagle feathers," he added after a shrewd glance at Good Plume's frowning face.

After some haggling, the trade was arranged, and Grass Heart came to live in Horse Runner's lodge. She was delighted, but he had no idea what to do with her; he had all the wives he could manage.

But she made herself useful, caring for the children of his lodge, making them new clothing which she decorated with novel paintings that pleased his wives and made the children laugh.

Winter threatened to come early to the plains, and the Sioux moved their camp to the hills far to the west.

Grass Heart walked behind a pony carrying large packs and dragging a travois on which rode two small children; a pair of fat puppies snuffled beside them. Sometimes children fell out of the travois and were lost, and it was her duty to see that none of Horse Runner's met with such a fate. She kept one eye on them, trudging alone across the vast plains, wearing patched moccasins and a warm capote against the sharp wind.

On the tenth morning, as the camp awoke and the usual confusion set in, she looked with awe on the blue line of mountains ahead of them, a jagged series of peaks and hills against the fresh, yellowing sky. It was the first time she had seen anything that tall and forbidding, and she felt dismayed at the thought of entering into the deep, dark timber stitched to their sides. Near a square butte, barren but for stunted pines, they crossed the last of the open land, moving up a narrow gulch that broadened out into a space where a stream ran and beaver ponds lay black and still under the heavy spruce boughs.

The air was sharp and thin; she took shallow breaths trying to draw it in. Smoke from the new fires rose upward in plumes that seemed to have no endings. The buffalo hide lodges were set up, bundles carried into them and unwrapped, and soon in the quick darkness that fell their triangular shapes became luminescent from the cooking fires burning within them. She stood on a hillside and thought them almost like ghostly lodges as the unseen flames grew and diminished.

A light snow fell before morning, and when she came out of the lodge the trees were white. A faint lace of ice rimmed the ponds. She took He Who Sees, the youngest child, to look at the pools, their footprints melting in the snow behind them. The boy squealed with delight and found pinecones to throw in the water. They floated there, making ripples that widened until gone.

A snowball lit at Grass Heart's feet. She looked up to find a young man standing among the trees. The child screeched, "Uncle!" and ran off to him. He lifted the boy to his shoulder.

"I am Kills Ree," he said.

The Sioux band he belonged to camped nearby, and he gave Horse Runner twenty fine ponies for Grass Heart, and she moved into his lodge. She was his first wife.

He was a man of many passions, and she was astonished at how they pleased one another. They laughed and wrestled in the warm furs of his bed, and often lay in the snow under a ledge, while the winter sun watched them with her pale eye. Her sexual enjoyment was as great as his, and their quarrels enthusiastic. She took to giggling for no apparent reason, and when her father came to visit her he watched her in disbelief.

Kills Ree gambled on anything: he was a superb rider, and when they held horse races he invariably won, and brought home many beautiful robes and pretty trinkets to her. She grew fat on her bones and he teased her, but liked to pinch her soft flesh and fondle her buttocks.

When he grew angry he was apt to tear apart the lodge in a noisy fury, and, once, when he carelessly cut his calf, he scandalized the entire village with his shouts and imprecations, tossing out into the mud the good iron teakettle he had given her.

She loved him with an intensity alien to her, but when she went with the other women for wood, climbing the steep hillsides, through dead falls, and over slippery needled rocks, she would look to the east, where the great river lay, and would wonder if she could ever return there, feeling a sickness in her heart she could not identify.

Good Plume found a small purple flower, cup-shaped, growing through the snow, and saw the bare patches widen around the trunks of the pines where their feet lay. He knew the sap was rising; and his own blood turned toward spring.

"Let us leave these people and go home," he told Grass Heart.

She was stirring food in the pot and dropped the spoon into the meat.

"Horse Runner will have us killed if we run away," she said.

"I have thought of that. What would Kills Ree do?"

"I don't know," she said, fishing out the spoon. Her father was sitting across the fire from her and she studied him. He looked old and forlorn, and the hair on his high skull was so scant and white it was hard to see. It came to her that he would die soon; he did not want to die among strangers; he had no one but herself to help him home to his village, to his own lodge, to the valley he loved so.

⌇

THEY MOVED AWAY FROM THE HILLS, wandering eastward, with Kills Ree's band. Horse Runner took his village south in search of fresh grass for the horse herds. He was not troubled at Good Plume's choice, only warning him again about the white man's treacherous ways, calling them "dog piss."

Kills Ree's party camped one day at the head of a stream that Good Plume recognized from his youth. It ran through cliffs banded with red and blue earth. He had been on an antelope trap there, and they had gotten so many of the animals their ponies weren't able to carry them all back to the river.

When Grass Heart told her husband that night what she was planning to do, he was silent for a long while, then got up from their bed and went out of the lodge. In the morning she found two horses staked beside the entrance.

"This horse is gentle," he said, slapping the flank of a red spotted mare. "Your father will find him easy to ride."

Tears filled the space behind her eyes. "How will I find you again?" she asked.

"The same way we found each other before," he laughed and put his dark narrow hand down the front of her dress. "Go," he said.

She had packed a few robes and some food, and they slept that first night in a heavy thicket of oaks. She did not sleep; she watched the stars wheel across the sky and wondered why Kills Ree had let her go so easily.

Good Plume claimed he could smell the big river when, at midday, they swung northward out onto a high land, cut deep with yellow clay coulees. He tried to force the big red spotted mare into a hard gallop, but she refused to change her rocking pace, snuffling as though to caution him to be patient.

When the sun reached the horizon to their backs, they rode out where the land dipped and saw, far off, the river, brown and swift and wide, in flood. It raced through the pale green track of the valley, and Good Plume cried out with joy at the sight of it.

At dusk they reached the village.

⌐

IN LATER YEARS, WHEN TELLING of his escape from the Sioux, Jake Moon glossed over much of it, leaving out how he had passed around Fort Pierre and evaded seeing Mrs. Rosen, to whom he owed money, and how he had made his way to St. Louis at last after many hardships.

And he never spoke of the nightmares he often suffered. In them he felt the rocking of the door as it floated down beyond the big bend in the river and saw the wall of trees fall behind, menacing enough in their silence. He had come out into a place of barren hills, covered with prickly bushes and pink-colored sand, where he found a ledge and went ashore, drawing the raft onto it.

He told of how he had no weapons but a knife and had found an ash tree from which he fashioned a spear. "Now I have two weapons," he said aloud, then looked about fearfully, not knowing whether anyone heard him.

When he reached the next stand of big timber he wove a rope of vines he gathered and interlaced with branches and wiry grass and made himself a low, shallow hut that he tied to his craft with strong reeds and more vines.

He endured a terrible storm and found refuge on a sandbar in the river, wrestling the heavy door up onto the sand where he lay, wet and shivering.

He became ill from the bite of some poisonous insect and cured himself of a fever with the juice of wild mint leaves, brewing it in a cedar bark cup over a fire he made with a bit of flintstone and his knife blade.

Everything he had learned from his year with the Mandans he put to good use, finding wild turnips and onions to eat, along with rabbits he trapped, or gophers netted from their burrows.

He lay up at first light under the washed-out banks of the river, drifting silently downward through the nights, passing Indian villages until he came at last to a trading post, a wretched place of logs covered with canvas. There he got drunk with the half-breed who owned it and was quite sick for several days, leaving behind him the door which he exchanged for a rude canoe. He carried with him a bad conscience and a monstrous headache, and arrived after other adventures in St. Louis, where he spent the rest of that winter and the whole of the next with a distant cousin, who gave him shelter and work.

⌐

JAKE MOON STOOD ON THE CORNER in front of the Great Western Saloon one fine spring day when he saw a familiar figure coming down the street.

If Carl Bessie had been sober he would have only nodded and passed on, but he held enough whisky in him to make him sociable; he stopped and looked inquiringly at the young man, recognizing him, although the face was pockmarked and older.

He snapped his fingers, saying, "From Fort Catherine, I saw you at Fort Catherine." There was certainly nothing wrong with *his* memory, he said to himself. Aloud, he said, "Have a drink with me."

"I would be pleased to," Jake Moon answered humbly.

Mr. Bessie steered him through the door, to a table by a window and, in a loud voice, called for a bottle and two glasses.

"How have you been?" he asked Jake, and hiccuped discreetly, as Jake began to describe the events that had occurred at Fort Catherine, dwelling on the horrors of the smallpox epidemic.

The artist turned quite pale. "I don't want to hear any more," he told Jake hurriedly and emptied his glass in one gulp. "It destroyed Lawrence Knipp, you know. He fell into disgrace with his employers over some matter concerning it that he would never discuss with me and was let go. He could find no other work, took to drink and died of it." His own hands trembled as he lifted his glass to his lips.

Jake was a bit shocked at the turn of events, remembering how he had wished the agent would suffer for his betrayal, leaving him behind as he had, and secretly felt avenged.

Mr. Bessie was looking out the window and Jake followed his gaze. Two women on the street were fighting, slapping wildly at one another, their bonnets fallen down their backs. It had rained in the night and the road was thick with mud. At last one slipped and fell from the wooden walk, sprawling backwards, drawing the other with her into the muck. The artist thought it a fitting end for such a spectacle and laughed, a raucous noise that startled Jake.

He asked about Father Bernard. Mr. Bessie said he had never met him, and Jake went on to tell of the part he had played in nursing the sick.

"The Indians probably got him," Mr. Bessie said indifferently and wiped his fingers on his vest.

Jake's tongue was loose from drink. "They could never get me, though they came close," he boasted.

While Bessie drank, Jake told of his escape downriver, omitting some of it and exaggerating other parts of it, especially those where through his knowledge of Indian craft he had been able to survive, thinking to himself that Mr. Bessie was owed something extra for the whisky he had bought him.

The artist turned his eyes fully on Jake; they were glassy and interested. "How would you like to guide an expedition I am setting up to the upper Missouri?" he asked.

"We haven't found anyone yet who we feel would be satisfactory, and with your knowledge of the country and its tribes I think you may be the man we are looking for. There are but three of us, not a large party, but we have arranged for an escort from Fort Snelling. We are authorized to gather specimens for scientific study." He stopped and peered out the low window, wishing the women would fight again, but they lay in the mud still, a crowd of people on the walk watching them. The women were smiling and kicking their heels in the air.

Later, when sober, he couldn't understand why he had made Jake the offer. He had not considered whether all that Jake Moon had told him was true, and he feared he had made a fatal mistake. Hopewell, the backer of the party, questioned him closely about Jake, and rather than admit he had made a hasty decision while under the influence of liquor, Bessie defended his choice.

"He knows the country, and he speaks the language. And he's had no formal education," he said, "an asset for us. He won't question what we do because he will have no interest in our research."

Reassured, Hopewell agreed, but warned against telling Jake any more than was necessary. "It wouldn't be wise," he said, "Dr. Stiles wants it private, he made that clear enough."

As for Jake, he had accepted the money Bessie had offered him when they left the tavern and watched the man leave, straying a little to the side as he walked carefully up the planked sidewalk, one foot stepping into the muddy street.

He understood he was to guide a party to the headwaters of the upper Missouri, and he had never been north of Fort Catherine. He felt confident. It was just a matter of following the river, he told himself jauntily, and went to outfit himself properly for the journey.

They left on the steamer *Marie Josephine* early in June and reached Fort Leavenworth where they met Dr. Stiles, a thin, surly man whom Jake took an instant dislike to. The doctor seldom spoke to him, and when he did his tone was arrogant. He was surprised to discover the man was not a doctor of medicine, but a botanist, so Hopewell told him, while Mr. Bessie called him a natural scientist. Both terms were beyond Jake's knowledge and he thought them dull sounding.

He learned that Mr. Hopewell was the man who was paying for the expedition, a brash, genial fellow who brought with him his personal cook, a black man named Hobie who turned out to be an excellent cook and good company.

Upriver, where they left the boat at Fort Snelling, Hopewell purchased wagons from a hostler, with sassy, delicate-footed mules to pull them. The wagons were high bodied, and iron-clad wheels, tall as a man, held them up. Jake thought them clumsy vehicles and was afraid he would be asked to drive one, but Mr. Bessie saw to it he was given a proper mount, a handsome, black beast that Jake fell in love with at once.

A man approached Mr. Hopewell one morning saying he was seeking employment as a teamster, that he had been working as one for the military but had been let go. He had heard of the expedition and waited for them to arrive. Mr. Hopewell hired him upon the recommendation of Bessie, who knew him, but when Jake saw him, he muttered darkly and refused to shake his hand.

"Frankie Paradise," said Hopewell. "He's signed on for the wagons," and left them.

"I know you," Jake said, "from Fort Catherine."

Paradise regarded him impudently, saying, "It give you scars enough."

In the room he had been given, Jake inspected his face in a bit of mirror tacked on the wall. His face was brown from the sun but pitted with white scars. From a box he took his new hat, one like he had admired on the French trappers in Fort Pierre, gay with ribbons. With it he wore his deerskin jacket; it had long fringes on the sleeves and when he went to supper that night he found them a considerable nuisance: he would forget and lift his arms too fast and the fringes struck him smartly in the face.

The day before they left Fort Snelling Mr. Hopewell held a final conference with the commandant, who assigned six soldiers to accompany the party on their travels. He also went to the office of the civil authorities, taking Jake with him.

A man dressed in a black suit so old it seemed rusty in the light from the dirty windows met them. He took them to a room at the side where another man waited behind a desk. While they chatted with Hopewell, Jake noticed the first man watching him anxiously, his eyes black like his clothing and rimmed with yellow rime. He turned his back and sat on a hard chair, counting the books on the shelves along the wall. There were a great many of them, some stamped with gold letters, and Jake wondered why so many were needed, here on the frontier. He bent forward to scan the titles, but could not make much sense of them and went back to studying the man with the strange eyes.

Jake decided he was a very sick man: it showed in his coloring, a pasty white, and in the manner in which his hands shook constantly. He took note of the shoes he wore, soft like a woman's, and recalled that when one had what was called in this territory the French Disease that the toes rotted away after the genitals became affected, so it was told, and he attempted to see if his teeth were gone too but the fellow kept his lips close together. In disgust, Jake left the room and waited for his employer on the stoop.

"It's all signed!" Hopewell cried when he came out, showing the signature beneath a seal of gold. "Now we are legal!"

Later, as they ate supper, Jake mentioned the thin man with the crusted eyes and gave his reasons for believing he had the French Disease. Mr. Hopewell said he understood him to be a minor judge, appointed by the government to serve the civilians at the fort, for he certainly wasn't military. And then he showed the paper to Dr. Stiles and Mr. Bessie, and mentioned the sick man's name. Bessie's face took on an unnatural light and he gleefully asked for a description, which Hopewell supplied, then was taken with such a fit of laughter he nearly choked to death, and was saved only by a hard pounding on the back by Dr. Stiles.

The name meant nothing to Jake; he was thinking how provident it was to have a doctor in the group, even though he was called a botanist or a naturalist—he still knew how to handle an emergency, such as Mr. Bessie had just undergone.

⌐

GRASS HEART AND HER FATHER found the village all but deserted, only a handful of old ones left: the crippled, the bedridden, the blind. They were slowly starving to death, the gardens grown to weeds, and no one able to hunt for meat.

They talked a bit to Good Plume about how the Hidatsa had come and offered to take the healthy ones back to their own village upriver. He returned to his lodge filled with gloom, clutching his breast. Grass Heart refused to be daunted; she scrounged for food from the empty lodges, digging in the caches left behind. She nagged Good Plume until he made new arrows for her from the chokecherry branches, and a short bow, and hunted the bottoms of the river where the deer and elk rested in the hot afternoons, bringing home meat on which they all feasted, those who could still eat.

But each week brought new deaths, the old ones giving up more from lack of will than from privation. She worried that her father would lose heart also and cheered him in every way she could devise. But winter hid just behind the horizon, coming closer each day; she could not hold back its approach.

The days grew shorter; the birds disappeared. Leaves turned copper and brown, and the wind began to bite. It rained then, long days and nights of rain, and she sat in the lodge, seeing her father grow gaunt and despondent. One night the sky cleared; fog hung in the valley. She lay in her ragged robe, hearing a hungry owl as it mocked the quarter moon. The fire was low and she rose and went to it, freshening it. Good Plume came from the shadows to sit by her.

"It is time we go," he said slowly. "We can't spend the winter here, with no meat or warm robes. My heart feels as empty as this village; I am as sad as the weather. I think, now, that I would welcome death, but for you. It is my fault you have no husband anymore. Let us leave here, go to the Hidatsa. There are people there who will give us a new life. The old one is all worn out."

A relative of Kills Ree, paunchy and middle-aged, had come soon after they had reached the village and reclaimed the horses, saying his nephew had sent him for them, and Grass Heart relinquished them after a bitter argument.

The rain had begun once more when they left the village. It beat against them as they wound along the narrow path up the hill toward the north, Grass Heart harnessed by leather thongs to a little sledge made of buffalo bones that held their few belongings.

Good Plume led, his third leg a crutch she had made from a forked branch. At the top of the hill they stopped and looked back. Neither spoke. The rain was like a door closing off the valley, and all in it, and they went on. A fox ran out before them, roused by their footsteps, red as flames, a sleek flash of scarlet, and she caught her breath at its beauty. She envied him.

She followed her father, hearing the sound of the foot of his crippled leg flapping on the muddy earth, and thought it the saddest sound in the world.

<hr/>

JAKE MOON STOOD UP IN HIS STIRRUPS and shouted "Forward!" and the expedition rode off to the west.

All were pleased at the ease with which the party passed through Indian country, seeing a few natives in the distance but none causing them trouble.

There were many lost miles in following the shores of the numerous lakes, and the sloughs and ponds that cut up the country, the water in the lakes as dark and deep as the center of the earth. Groves of trees hung motionless on the horizon, and along the trail a variety of flowers lay bright-colored.

Then the country began to slope, and creeks and rivers appeared, which they forded without difficulty. No untoward incidents disturbed their journey, and Jake gave grudging credit to Frankie Paradise and a soldier by the name of Coleman, both of whom had made the trip across this vast prairie, from Fort Catherine to Fort Snelling, two summers past.

They stopped often for Dr. Stiles to pick flowers and look at bones.

Jake thought he showed a nasty interest in the Indian burial scaffolds they encountered, but had no idea what he did among them, for he was kept busy setting up the camps and planning the next day's march. Mr. Bessie and Stiles seemed to spend an inordinate amount of time going through the bones on the platforms; the rest of the party shied away from them, even though they held only dead Indians.

Fort Catherine was still intact. There had been another attempt to burn it: the timbers were badly charred where some of the store rooms had been fired. After surveying it, Hopewell said they would camp in the courtyard. "I don't care to sleep under a roof when I can do it under the stars," he said. Dr. Stiles agreed. It made little difference to him where he slept, he said, but Bessie privately would have liked more security.

After a meal of antelope steaks, Jake Moon went up on the wall to look at the sunset, carefully picking his way, the ladder rotted from the weather. He rested his arms on the parapet, seeing the rounded tops of the village across the river, black beneath the western hills where gold streaked the crest. He had brought a spyglass with him and through it saw weeds growing on the roofs. It gave him an eerie feeling. Nothing moved but an eagle, swinging in a wide circle over the river, the sky growing the pale purple color he remembered so well, fading to a pearly green, then dusk. He stood there until full dark and spoke to no one when he went to his bed.

The next morning they hoisted the flag on the pole and breakfasted on freshly killed quail.

⌒

"I CAN'T SMOKE THE TOBACCO," Good Plume said. "It hurts my throat."

The Hidatsa grew poor tobacco, short-leafed and bitter. They smoked it raw, since no red willows grew near their village for bark to mix it with.

"You have smoked it all winter," answered Grass Heart. She was scraping a deerskin with a bit of horn she had sharpened. Flies and gnats from a pile of offal nearby hung over her. She had let her hair hang loose to protect her face from them, and now she brushed it back with a hand dark with dried blood. Sweat ran from her armpits; her back hurt from stooping.

"It isn't far," he wheedled, "we can get there in a day, and I can find enough in the old gardens for my own use. You know how tall it grows and how hard it is to kill off, even when the first frost comes."

"I don't want to go," she said. "Maybe there is none growing there anymore; maybe we would go all that way for nothing."

"I will go alone." He hardened himself against the stricken look in her eyes. "Or we can ride the horses and go together."

He had acquired two ponies that their owners no longer wanted: one had taken an arrow in the eye, so was useless, and the other wore a strange growth along the side of a rear leg. The Hidatsa medicine man had asked too much to treat it, and Good Plume traded a buffalo robe for the pair of them.

He fixed a blanket cover for the afflicted animal. It lay over its back, hanging to the knees and hiding the tumor. He gave the eyeless one to Grass Heart, for it was cautious and safer to ride. She had always been reckless when riding, and on this animal he thought no harm could come to her.

She continued her scraping, her head bent, and he regarded her from half-closed eyes. He drew on his pipe and coughed gently. When she looked up he smiled.

"One day with the horses," he said, then limped into the lodge and brought out his new horn bow, the quiver of arrows, and a long iron-bladed lance. These and a knife and a hatchet he laid down before her, the seams of his face crooked with smiling. "Here," he said, "if we meet the Sioux."

"Wrong time of the summer for them," she said. "You are crazy. What if we meet with white men?"

"I will kill them," Good Plume said.

The morning sun lay atop the cottonwoods lining the Knife River when they left. The smell of sweetgrass and horse filled his high nose. Visibly he grew taller in the wooden saddle, and often he scratched at his ear, a sign he was happy. Yellow-legged grouse strutted in the plum thickets, whistling, and Grass Heart began to sing, a high, thin falsetto that sent them dodging away. Soon they came in sight of the big river and turned southward; it wound, brown as a snake, with no shine to its skin, but she could smell it and felt her heart swell behind her ribs.

There was no need this time to stay on the path. The horses picked their way over the prairie, the one-eyed pony's head lying next to the other's flank. By late afternoon they were following the hill north of the old village.

Suddenly Grass Heart pulled at the rope bridle of her horse. "I can see smoke," she said. "There." And pointed in the direction of the fort.

She helped her father dismount. They led the animals below the crest and crept up to look down toward the village. Nothing moved there.

At last Good Plume spoke. "White men," he said, and she nodded her head.

"It is too far to go back to the Hidatsa before dark, not with these horses. We can make a camp, without a fire, and stay the night where we are and leave before the sun comes," Grass Heart mused, "or else we can go the back way to the village, to see if the old ones there have come to any harm.

"I would not feel right if we ran away without knowing how it is with them," she continued. She felt there was little danger and was certain her father would forgo his search for tobacco, with the white men so near.

Making a circle, they entered the rear gates to the village, finding it empty as they searched through the lodges, apparently vacant for some time, for the dust lay heavy on the floors and the fire pits held old ashes.

In one lodge the body of an old woman rested in a shroud of skins, and when Grass Heart uncovered the face she did not recognize it, but Good Plume said it was Lone Woman, the wife of Long Catcher, uncle of Sweet Flag, and she wondered what had become of Bloody Dog, berdache, her childhood love, and snorted in disbelief that she could have been so young and foolish as to pursue him as she had, that she had been married twice and was now in her seventeenth summer, had survived the smallpox epidemic, been enslaved, traveled to the Black Hills and back, rescued her father from the pesthouse and cared for him ever since, while, as Sweet Flag, he had lived a useless, empty life, vulgar and trivial. Then she remembered his sweet smile and gentle manner when he explained to her how his blood ran in another direction, and pushed all memories of him from her mind, with regret, watching her father cover Lone Woman's face, his hands spotted with age and trembling from fatigue.

They stabled the horses in the lodge and ate a cold meal, talking of little. Good Plume sat in the doorway with his weapons as darkness fell, and she heard his muffled snores from her robe. Before first light she rose and wakened him. They led the horses out of the village and hid them in a grove of trees, climbing to the top of the cliff, south beyond the gardens.

Grass Heart brought stones from the creek bed and built a wall of them around a ledge, where they lay concealed. The river lay below, rose-streaked with the dawn. Across it the flag rippled in the morning wind, and Good Plume felt his heart trying to leave his body and held it down with both hands.

With the sun fully risen, she could see the white men's camp in the square and the wagons and men stirring about.

"There seem to be only a few. There's no boat and no guards. I think it is only some hunters," she said. "They won't cause any trouble. We can leave if you are ready."

"I am in no hurry," he told her, "there's plenty of time to get my tobacco. I didn't come all this way to look at white men."

She faced away from the river, ready to argue with him, when he slapped his knee and laughed, saying, "Dog-pissers, that's what Horse Runner called them. And, see, they come this way!"

Five men with a packhorse were riding to the riverbank, and she felt a slow rage rise in her throat. Pulling her father to his feet she pushed him from their little den; he stumbled over the rocks, then ran behind her to the grove where the horses waited.

⌒

JAKE MOON SAID, "Do you want to see the village today?" looking unconcerned when Bessie shot him a glance he could not read.

Coleman and Paradise already sat on their horses; a pack animal was tied behind Coleman's mount, boxes strapped across its back. The animal whinnied when Dr. Stiles approached, a loud liquid sound, and he gave it a slashing blow across its nose with his whip.

Jake had noticed before how cruelly he treated the animals of the party, refusing to watch when he struck the thin-skinned mules until welts rose on their backs and their legs bowed out as they fought the reins.

"We can take a quick look at it if Dr. Stiles wants," said Bessie, his saddle giving a long croak as he put his weight into it. "I don't think there would be much of interest in it."

"I don't expect it's been lived in for some time," Jake said. "Not since the smallpox."

Dr. Stiles had oddly green eyes, and he fastened them on Bessie, who was leaning forward, trying to settle himself more securely in the saddle. "Hasn't Mr. Bessie said anything to you about the purpose of our trip?" he asked Jake.

"Of course he did. He told me you came here for birds and plants and such things." Jake resented the offensive tone with which Stiles addressed him and thought: You would never have gotten this far if it hadn't been for my experience.

Stiles shrugged airily. "Well, we can take a short look, then see to the other."

The day after their arrival Hopewell had taken to his cot with a fever. Dr. Stiles had dosed him with laudanum, and he drifted in and out of uneasy sleep, hearing Hobie whistling in the cook tent. Two of the soldiers slept in the shade of the wall; the others he had no knowledge of, nor cared to. The sun's heat was oppressive; he sweated profusely; cooler, sweeter climates drifted in his head. He woke once to see Hobie drinking from a bottle. The black man set it down and began to saw at his toenails with his butcher knife. Hopewell closed his eyes.

The red-haired soldier Rafferty came from the mule yard and glared at Hobie. Rafferty hated "niggers," especially Hobie, who held a special position among the party.

He found his fellow soldiers, Joe and Andy, stretched out alongside the wall, and out of boredom they agreed to go with him to the river for a swim.

Out of sight of the fort, they wandered downstream, searching for a place away from the main current, finding at last a still pool under some trees. A she-bear with cubs lay on the sandy bank, the cubs playing in the shallows, splashing and squealing like children. Andy suggested they move closer; he was fascinated by the brown, shining animals, and although Rafferty cautioned them against getting too close the three men left the trees, edging out toward the water.

The sow lifted her head and sniffed. Swiftly she reared up to her full height and charged. Frozen with shock, the men could not move, and she sprang on Joe, tearing out his throat, and lifted Andy in her arms, breaking his back. Rafferty heard it snap and saw him fall, then heard her roaring as she sank her teeth into the helpless man.

In blind panic he ran toward the cliffs, looking back when he reached them to see her dragging the body about, mauling it with her fierce claws. He scrambled up the rocks, stopping only when he thought he could go no farther, his breath ragged. Hanging by his hands he looked down. The cubs and the sow were gone. He closed his eyes and rested his chin on a ledge.

Something struck him on the cheek. For an instant he thought it an insect, then it struck again, and he saw what it was, its skin just shed lying beside it like a piece of crumpled brown paper, a string of round rattles dangling from it.

His throat closed up and the white sky darkened abruptly.

⌐

THE FOUR MEN REACHED THE VILLAGE by taking the old ford below it, Jake showing them where it was. As they reached the tumbled-down palisades, Stiles gave the ruins a contemptuous look and said, "I thought your famous Mandan kept their villages neat." Bessie tried to explain the village was abandoned, but Stiles paid him no attention.

Jake left them examining the council lodge and went to find Good Plume's lodge. He found signs it had recently been occupied and discovered near the fire pit an old bent fork that Grass Heart had once used. He put it in his pocket. The lodge held a musty smell, and a spider had crisscrossed the smoke hole with a shimmering web that caught nothing but the sun. The dimness and the arching dome above him gave him a feeling that was unpleasant; he was too warm in his deerskin coat, and he eased it off, folding it over his arm.

Frankie had waited at the gate, holding the horses, and Jake went there and felt over his horse's pack, strapping it down firmly. His red flannel shirt shone with grease he had spilled on it, and the armpits were wet with dark rings. He envied the canvas vest Stiles had worn; its pockets sagged with tools. Coleman looked the coolest of them all in a lightweight blue shirt.

Bessie had his pipe going when Jake returned to where they stood, and Dr. Stiles was staring into the distance, his mind on other things than empty villages.

"Which direction is it?" he asked Bessie. Jake wiped the sweat from his brow. The sun stood at noon, and his stomach growled softly.

"I recall seeing them in those trees, there," Bessie answered with reluctance. "See, there past what were the gardens, past those huge rocks and the cliff. You turn and go up the little creek that runs along there, then you come to the big woods. Jake told me in one of those hillsides they buried a lot of them, but it's covered over with rocks and most likely hard to find." He was strangely uneasy and would not look at Jake, who moved nearer.

Stiles said they should walk to the garden area, that at least they would be more shaded beyond it. He led the way, Jake at the rear. A badger peered from a hole where a wall once stood, his little eyes spiteful, and Jake threw a rock at it to drive it away. They passed the fences that marked the gardens, the rough slats broken and tipped, some gone altogether. He looked down to the river. The sun had drowned in its silted depths.

They stopped under the shade of the aspen. Shadows from the leaves dappled their faces. "Where next?" Stiles asked Jake.

"Where what?" said Jake, bewildered.

Bessie cleared his throat. "Dr. Stiles wants to see where these Indians put their dead."

⌐⌐

I SHOULD HAVE KNOWN, thought Jake, recalling the man's unnatural interest in the scaffolds on the prairies, and with the hollowing behind the ribs he said, "I don't know if I could find the place; I was only there one time and it was coming on to dark, nearly, and I was in a hurry."

"You were hired on as a guide on the basis of your specific knowledge of these people on this part of the river." Dr. Stiles set his formidable eyes on those of Jake's. "You are to fulfill your duties, as expected. You have been quite voluble to Mr. Bessie, giving all sorts of details as to how they lived. I assume you also know what became of them when they died." He turned to Coleman. "Tell that Paradise fellow to bring the horses."

They rode through the grove, across the sparkling creek, and into the woods, Jake at the head of the party. Ancient cottonwoods, huge and dark of leaf, enclosed the earth, branches as large as ordinary tree trunks, wrapped with dead vines, making an endless canopy over a floor of moss and dead leaves swallowing the sounds they made.

No birds sang in its gloom; no small animals scurried from their approach. Through deep shadow they moved; but for the jingle of harness and a furtive snort from Jake's black horse, the quiet was unbroken. He thought of ghosts and spirits and gave an involuntary shudder. Even Frankie Paradise seemed affected, and Bessie drew in his breath as though sipping a bitter liquid. Only Dr. Stiles appeared unmoved, saying, in a normal voice, "We'll dismount here. Take the horses back to the creek.

Let them drink. We shall be here for some time," and Frankie obeyed, leaving only the packhorse behind.

Coleman led it by its bridle as they walked farther into the woods. All at once Stiles stopped short and pointed up at a tree.

"There's one," he said, satisfaction coloring his voice.

It was a long box, wedged into the lower branches of a tree. He motioned to Jake. "Get Coleman to help you lift it down."

Jake looked to Bessie. The man was standing with his legs apart, his red face lifted up, blank eyes staring at the coffin, and Jake saw his jaw hanging open and thought, this is how he will look when he is dead.

He did not want to touch the coffin; he wanted to say it was wrong, even sinful. The wooden box meant someone of great honors rested there: ordinary Indians were not given such care; they were sewn in skins, then wrapped in hides, all sewn tightly around them, and placed in a fork of a tree. He could see the bundles among the low branches, scraps of blanket and bright cloth hanging from them. This wooden box must have been a famous chief, he told himself, and wished he had never come here.

"Get it down," ordered Stiles.

Being the smaller and lighter of the two, Jake stood on Coleman's shoulders and freed the box from its perch, finding it much easier than he had guessed it would be. Panting, he lowered it to Dr. Stiles, who snarled, "Be careful, you fool! Don't drop it."

Bessie, startled from his trance, removed a small crate from the packhorse and laid it beside the doctor. He was horrified by the eagerness with which Stiles attacked the lid of the coffin with a small iron bar. It gave a faint squeal and he lifted it, sliding it to one side.

Without wanting to, Bessie leaned over and looked.

"What do you think?" Stiles asked. "Unusually well preserved, I would say."

And he reached down into the coffin. "The head still has its hair." His voice seemed to come from the box itself, like a secret.

Jake saw the muscles of his arms moving under the canvas vest. He made a wrenching motion, and his hands came up holding the head. Stringy hair dangled over a partially fleshed skull that grinned from a slack jaw as he held it aloft.

⤙

IN THE DEEPEST PART OF THE WOODS Grass Heart rested, watching her father's breast rise and fall as he slept.

His leg had given way before they reached the aspen grove and the horses, and she had helped him here, where they hid, and now he slept, his white hair shining against the moss his head lay on.

The jingle of metal and hooves clicking on the rocks along the creek had given them warning, and the faint murmur of voices not far off told her the white men had come into the woods. With a hand across his lips she woke Good Plume; silently they moved from tree to tree, the lance held close to her breast. He carried his bow, the quiver ready at his shoulder, the hatchet safe in her belt.

Afterwards, she could recall little of how it happened: she remembered hearing the twang of the bowstring and turning her head to see Good Plume fit another arrow to its notch. "No," she hissed in horror and clutched at his arm.

"They are taking White Cow's head," he said.

Jake had been standing by the coffin when Stiles took a strange instrument from a pocket of his coat and fitted it around the skull. He averted his gaze in time to see Coleman grasp at a stick protruding from his shirt, his face blank with disbelief. Then the soldier folded his arms around it; he hugged his death like a lover, saying "Husssh, husssh," and fell to earth.

At almost the same instant Jake felt a heavy blow take him in the shoulder, looked down and saw the arrow shaft, its yellow feathers bright against his red shirt. They moved with his breath.

Carl Bessie dropped the skull. Stiles dove for Coleman's gun and had almost reached it when Grass Heart stepped out behind him.

His broad back filled her eyes. She drove the blade of the lance into it, ramming it through the canvas, flesh, tissue, hesitating for but an eye blink as it nicked bone, then as the man dropped the haft swung upward, striking her cheek. The long, slim shaft hummed in the sudden silence.

She looked at Carl Bessie. "Pick up the head," she told him.

He could not move. She bent down and lifted the skull, reverently, laying it back in the coffin. Jake was still staring at Stiles, whose body hung suspended on the lance, the spearhead in the ground. The green eyes studied the uncaring earth.

Good Plume stood in the shadows, the empty bow in his hand. "Why did you want to kill me?" asked Jake in wonder.

Grass Heart stepped between them. "I think he knew you at the last instant, or you would be dead like the soldier," she said.

"Why kill him?" Jake gestured at the man hanging on the lance.

"He is a thief, a robber of the dead," Grass Heart told him. She went to him and touched the arrow in his shoulder.

"Ahh, old friend, why did you bring these men here to steal from us."

"I didn't know, I swear I didn't know what they meant to do." Tears glazed his blue eyes.

"Go home, Jake Moon. Go home. It's over now, don't come again. You bring death with you each time you come." She took her father by the hand and melted into the forest.

"MR. BESSIE! WAKE UP, IT'S JAKE!" he urged the artist, shaking him with his good arm, but the man still stood beside the coffin. Jake took the pry bar and hammered down the lid, avoiding looking inside, then grasped Bessie by the arm and walked him toward the creek.

Paradise was sitting on the bank, tossing pebbles into the clear water, and rose as they came up, his mean face alive when he spied the arrow shaft. He saw where Mr. Bessie had wet himself, the front of his trousers dark from urine.

"Indians," was all Jake would tell him, and he hurried to help Bessie into a saddle, and Jake to mount, and hurried them away from the woods toward the river, the reins of their horses clutched in his fist.

Hopewell heard the shouts coming from the river and sat up in alarm.

"Hobie!" he yelled, "get the soldiers!"

Before the black man could comply, the horses came charging through the gates.

Paradise's face was white as he jumped to the ground, and Bessie slumped forward in his saddle with both hands holding to the horse's mane. It took both of them to pry them loose, the animals dancing about in excitement.

Hopewell was baffled at Bessie's behavior: he mumbled unintelligently about Indians and was so distraught that Hopewell gave up. Seeing no other solution, he ordered Hobie to stun the man, hoping to shock him into normality. The Negro took up a heavy frying pan and struck Bessie hard on the head. He dropped neatly to the ground.

"Oh Christ," said Hopewell, "you probably killed him."

All this while Jake Moon sat quietly on his horse, holding his injured shoulder. Paradise returned with the two soldiers, one dragging a string of fish behind him, and eased Jake down. Meanwhile Hobie had covered Bessie with a blanket and came to tend to Jake. He poured whisky into the wound after trying to draw out the arrow, then swiftly lifted the bottle to his own lips, drinking deeply, and retreated to the cook shack where he waited for the Indians to attack the camp, a meat cleaver in his tremulous hands.

Hopewell put Jake under the blanket with Bessie and turned to Paradise. "What happened?" he said.

The man related as well as he could what had led to their flight, while the two soldiers gathered up the guns and set up a barricade before one of the untouched storerooms. The unconscious Bessie was carried into the room and Jake helped there also, then Hobie, half-drunk but docile.

As the day rode over the hills with the sun, Bessie slept on. Jake sat apart, the only one who knew there would be no further bloodshed.

"You said an old Indian and a girl?" asked Hopewell. "You are sure?"

"I never seen 'em, but that's what Mr. Bessie said afore he went to pieces on me."

"But how do we know there aren't more of them? I can't see how only two of them got so close and surprised you all so easily!"

"I said I never seen 'em," Paradise said defensively. "It's what Mr. Bessie said. He even told their names but they went right out of my head in all the mess we was in."

"Hobie!" called Mr. Hopewell, "come here with that bottle."

They shared what was left, although Paradise refused to drink after Hobie unless he wiped the bottle clean with a cloth, and even made a show of wiping it himself with his own dirty handkerchief from his neck.

"Where's Rafferty and them others?" he asked suddenly.

The soldier called Briscoe shook his head dumbly. "They meant to go swimming," he said, "but they never come back."

"Well, we'll see in the morning. Get some sleep for now. But fix it so we trade off watches," he said.

He thought of all there was to do: get Dr. Stiles's and Coleman's bodies out of the woods and set up a search for the missing soldiers. Find the girl and the old man, if they really existed. Decide how they should be punished.

The idea of instant justice repelled him; ordinary men had no right to it, rather it fell to the proper authorities of this country to measure it out, he believed. He vowed that if he and the men caught them he would take them to Fort Snelling. He knew himself to be a fair-minded, responsible citizen and would act accordingly.

⤸

TO AVOID HER EYES, Good Plume adjusted the rope bridle, saying, "I have plenty of time."

He seemed much recovered; he was alert, and some of the old vigor showed in his movements as he fooled with the rein.

"I haven't gotten what I came for," he said and pointed to the pipe hanging about his neck. "I'll slip into the garden, take but a little, and you go on." He was already mounted and before she could stop him he had kicked the crippled horse into a trot. "I will meet you north of the village," he called as he rode away.

Angrily, she swung her horse to intercept him, and the half-blind animal, his empty eye unseeing of the tree before him, crashed into it, falling to his knees. She was pitched headlong into the rocks, and lay there a moment, stunned. By the time she had gotten to her feet and stopped the pony's trembling, Good Plume was gone. She ran to the rocks, climbed them, and looked toward the gardens.

He was there, astride his horse, surrounded by white men.

⌐

HOPEWELL HAD BEEN MUCH RELIEVED when Bessie awoke with nothing more than a raging headache. Jake lay in his blanket, his gaze inward.

"Do you remember what happened?" Hopewell asked Bessie, speaking in a low voice.

"I tried to persuade Stiles not to disturb their dead, but he insisted on going to that place, he was bent on getting a head from there," Bessie answered and rubbed his forehead distractedly.

"You told Paradise their names; you knew them, the old man and the girl." The man's voice was accusing, and Bessie bravely lied: "I couldn't have known them, I don't remember that part at all."

"They killed Dr. Stiles and Coleman and deserve to be punished."

Jake wished he could hear what was being said. Paradise moved closer and broke in to say, "You did so tell me you knew them, and they must of knew you, else you'd be dead too."

Hopewell decided he did not like the teamster's manners, nor the tone of his voice. "Well, Mr. Bessie has had a bad shock. His memory is somewhat confused as to the events. We'll leave him alone. You get the horses and we'll go for the bodies. Get Talley to help you."

"And catch them Indians," said Paradise. "If we hurry we can find 'em, they can't git far, a girl and a old man, didn't have no horses."

Briscoe and Talley, the other soldier, had been conferring together and came up to where Hopewell stood. "What about Rafferty and Joe and Andy? Think they was ambushed too?"

"Naw," Paradise said, giving emphasis to the word. "I think they jest took off, deserted. Joe told me he didn't want no part of this duty."

Talley seemed in agreement, for he nodded his head, looking wise.

"Could be," he said. "Could be Joe talked the others into it."

No one thought to look for the missing soldiers' horses; they were cropping contentedly in the small pasture behind the stables with the hobbled mules. Their own were tied to the railing of a porch, close at hand during the night, and Paradise went to untie them.

"Let's go now, before it gets any lighter," Hopewell told them, strapping on his gun. No one could fault him as being a coward, he thought. "Keep good watch, Hobie," he said. "And put fresh wrappings on Jake's arm. Carl, you keep out of the sun."

He felt he had done all he could and swung aboard his horse, the three men following him, their rifles glinting in the early light, the packhorse now unburdened, straining in their wake, the river washing up around his belly, as they crossed it to the other side.

Good Plume heard their hoofbeats. He waited, knowing they would soon see him, his heart falling to the earth.

It was as good a time to die as any.

⌐

GRASS HEART SAW THEM TIE HIM to his horse and lead him to the river. How tall he sat, how splendid his high skull, towering over the others, his white hair shining in the sunlight!

At dusk, she crossed the river, far to the south. She needed the cover of the night to move, unobserved, and reached the fort before the moon rose, leading her horse the final way. Muzzling him, she snubbed him to a tree and crept to the walls.

She knew every foot of the fort: its corners, the narrow porches, how to reach the roofs, which were safe and which to avoid, and where to find the forgotten door. In the yard, beyond the firelight, she spied Good Plume, tied to a post by thongs about his wrists. He appeared to be asleep, and she lay listening to the men.

They discussed how they had buried the bodies where they found them, not having either the heart or stomach to move them, since the heat had fouled their corpses and the animals had been at them during the night.

Traveling on to Fort Union was mentioned, but none of the men wanted to go upriver; they argued that they were too few, that other Indians might be lurking nearby, and the man called Hopewell did not argue very strongly for it.

"It's close, not far off," he said, "but dangerous, I believe. At least we know the trail back to Fort Snelling, and it is logical to return there."

"We will take but two of the wagons; one for the prisoner and the other for what we can salvage of our own baggage. It means leaving behind the doctor's specimens, but it can't be helped. There aren't enough of us to handle everything." He sighed in despair. "Briscoe, you drive one wagon, and I'll drive the other, and we will take extra horses in case we have Indian trouble on the way."

One of the soldiers suggested they would have to kill the old Indian, if others attacked them, and Bessie protested, saying, "I am aware it may be necessary, but meanwhile I expect all of you to treat our prisoner well. I, for one, understand why he did what he did," and refused to explain any further.

By daylight, Grass Heart was miles to the east, her father's horn bow and quiver riding her shoulders. It puzzled her why the men had left those things lying over the saddle of his horse. Even more curious had been the action of Hopewell. Before retiring, he had untied the animal from the railing and turned it loose. She had caught it easily and removed the weapons, all but the hatchet.

Now the bowstring was snug inside her gown, against the night dew. In a coulee she let her horse crop at the dry grass while she ripped with a knife the beads from her dress and her moccasins, and the bright quillwork from her sleeves. She buried them all in an ant-hill, then smoothed dust over her hair to keep it dull, and lay on the lip of the cutbank, watching the west, only the white mark in her eye distinguishing her from the earth itself.

⌐

FRANKIE PARADISE AND BRISCOE TOOK THE BARS from the former jail of the fort. Under the collapsed floor of the old blacksmith shop they found several coils of heavy chains. They made a rude cage in one of the wag-ons, fastened together with the chains, and put Good Plume into it, pil-ing those bars that were left on top of him.

Bessie was highly indignant, but Hopewell sided with the soldiers, knowing it wiser to bend somewhere, to keep them friendly and obedi-ent, for they did not like the idea of transporting the prisoner and grumbled about it.

Hopewell pointed out that it was for the protection of all to cage the man, and if they met unfriendly Indians the story of the cage and chains would spread through the prairie tribes and perhaps dampen their en-thusiasm for warring on the travelers.

When the men went for the mules they found the pretty animals gone and also most of the horses. Talley found a piece of the fencing torn out and quarreled with Paradise about it, leading to blows. They fought until Hopewell came and separated them.

The traveling was slow, the horses hitched to the wagons not fitted for such work, and they stopped often to let them rest. Then a prairie fire burned to the north, far off, gray smoke clouds hugging the land, burn-ing their eyes and throats. They found a buffalo wallow and waited there until the fire passed. Hobie fell sick from the bad water he drank there, making Hopewell despair.

All during this time Jake Moon stayed away from the caged Indian; he dared not admit familiarity with him but spent time scheming how to set him free without bringing blame onto himself. His arm ached from where Hopewell had finally removed the arrow. Often he wished he had never come west.

⤸

TO SPEED THEM ON THEIR RETURN, the next evening they abandoned one of the wagons and, double-teamed, eased the other with its cage down into a small canyon where a series of pools lay like dirty beads in its bottom. Hopewell and Bessie carried what they could from the abandoned wagon and piled it on the sand below the cliffs.

Asking the men to sit down, Hopewell spoke. "We are in bad straits, I think. I'm not as familiar with the country as I thought and will have to rely on Frankie Paradise to help us through this."

"In another five or six days we would have gotten near that trading post on the Red River. Now I want you, Paradise, and Briscoe here, to ride on ahead and get help there. At any cost. I'll pay whatever they ask, but get help."

Talley began to whine that they would starve before help would reach them, and an argument ensued about food. They had seen no game for some time, and the Indian had reduced their supply drastically.

"We're already on half-rations," he groused, and Hopewell said they would go on half that, so the two men could get through for help.

"Then don't feed that old Indian," said Paradise. "I starve and he eats. It's me doin' the dangerous job while he sits comfortable and has food brung to him."

"I want to talk to you privately," Hopewell told him and drew him aside. He took from his pocket a packet of money, gold from the sound of it, Paradise thought.

"Use it to get help," said Hopewell.

Very little escaped Briscoe's sharp eyes; he saw the packet given and received, and hastily tucked into the teamster's shirt. And he was the only one who saw Paradise slip a bottle from Hobie's tent, hiding it under his arm. He was waiting, already mounted, and gave a secret smile when Paradise swung into his saddle, the bottle safe in a saddlebag.

Hopewell watched them leave, his anxious eyes watching until they disappeared, turning them on Hobie, who lay apart, his skin gray, his face sickly. Talley sat nearby.

"If any Indians are out there and want us they'll know we're in this canyon. That goddamn wagon up there stands out like a red flag," he advised Hopewell.

He refused to help in any way, and Hopewell walked up over the cliff with an ax. He chopped it up as best he could and set it afire.

Talley told him, "That's a stupid idea, now it's like a beacon, all that smoke, see it clear to the mountains."

Hopewell told him to shut his mouth; he was exhausted. He ached with fatigue. His body protested the lack of food. He noticed the soldier saunter off toward the wagon with the cage, knowing what he had in mind, but too worn out to do anything other than turn his head away, shame replacing fear. He felt he was living in a nightmare with no ending.

As for Jake Moon, he saw nothing. He slept as though dead.

⌒

GRASS HEART BORE ANOTHER KIND of pain. Her horse had stumbled, throwing her to earth, and when she looked she found blood flowing from her leg. Wiping it away with a corner of her skirt, she saw a long, open gash. She wrapped it with a bit of doeskin cut from her dress, finding she could walk.

The horse lay on its side, the blank socket open to the sky. There was no breath coming from the thick lips. The quiver was torn, the arrows scattered. She found three unbroken ones and the bow, fallen in the deep grass, unharmed.

The wagon tracks showed her the way, and she set out on foot, walking until dark, when she could no longer see the trail. She slept while the stars burned in the endless sky, and wolves talked from the grass.

On the third day after the death of her horse, the sun fell in a splash of color, a halfway moon showing in the east. The ripe grasses sang with the evening wind, a wind that carried on it a breath of smoke.

She had found them.

She went onward. Mist rose from the land as it cooled; shadows formed, and summer lightning sent enormous flags of blue and yellow across the northern sky. The smell of smoke grew stronger, and she came upon the glowing embers of the wagon. Scanning the earth around it she found tracks and followed them to the edge of a cliff. On her belly she looked downward and saw a campfire and heard men talking.

Only white men would hide in a canyon, she thought, and make a fire and talk so loud.

She let her eyes close.

⌒

AT FIRST BRISCOE WAS ANGRY because Frankie Paradise wouldn't share the whisky; then he told himself he didn't care, he would stay sober. Let the son of a bitch drink himself silly; he wanted to get out of this country.

They rode through the night, and when the sun stuck her red eye over the prairie Paradise tried to shoot it out, laughing crazily, and it was then the soldier decided he would go no farther with him, let alone as far as the trading post.

Briscoe thought of the packet of money in the man's shirt. I could go a long ways with that, he thought, and slowed his horse to a walk, falling in behind him.

He lifted his rifle and sighted it, squeezing the trigger with a precise finger.

The gold felt heavy and fine against his own skin as he remounted.

"To hell with you," he said to the fallen Paradise, "and to hell with Hopewell and the rest."

↜

JAKE WAS STANDING BY THE BLACK HULK when he heard, faintly, what he thought was a rifle shot on the wind. He had been looking at a footprint he had found—a moccasin shape—and stooped to study it. If anything crossed his mind at the sound of the shot it was that Briscoe or Paradise had found game, and he continued studying the print.

It had to be Mandan, he decided, baffled, then thought it might be Sioux, and vowed not to mention it to Hopewell.

Jake's wound was healing at last. He could not use the arm as freely as he wished, and spent a good deal of time resting.

After they had moved down into the canyon, he managed to talk to Good Plume. Jake had never considered the old man an enemy in spite of the killings in the woods. Dr. Stiles had deceived him, attempting to steal the head of a great chief. It was hard to reconcile the death of Coleman, though, but he could not blame Good Plume; it must have been a dreadful shock to him, the sight of White Cow's skull being lifted from the coffin.

Good Plume apologized to Jake for shooting him, saying some good spirit had turned his aim at the last instant, to put the arrow in his arm instead. He also told Jake that Grass Heart had gone on ahead of him, to the Hidatsa village, and was safe there.

Then Hopewell came along and caught him, and told him to stay away from the prisoner, that Talley was responsible for him and brought him food and water each day. He needed no other attention, he said.

But Talley visited oftener than seemed necessary, staying a while when fetching water, and Jake thought him a kind man.

And now there was the moccasin print.

⌐

SOMETHING WOKE GRASS HEART. She snaked on her belly to the edge of the cliff. A dry stream bed, gray as an old rope, marked the depth of the canyon. Little pools of water winked at her in the dim light of dawn.

A fire burned among the black trees, smoke rising in feathers to the sky. Fear gripped her heart: they had gone while she slept; then a horse whinnied and her spirit lifted with the sun.

The gash in her leg had opened again, and fresh blood stained the wrapping. Somewhere she had lost a moccasin. She removed the other, indifferent now to anything but what lay below.

A ledge jutted from the cliff halfway down, and she cut grass with her knife and slid down, making a nest there. Cross-legged she sat and tested the bowstring. The three arrows, feathered with death, she lay beside the bow.

Her swollen tongue reminded her she had no water, and she wondered if her father felt thirst too, and sucked on a pebble.

How many days had she spent riding at night through the cutbanks of the coulees, out of sight of the sun, keeping beneath the rim of the earth, walking and running to catch up after losing her horse, eating wild roots or snared prairie dog? She didn't know. It was all timeless. Now it was nearing the end.

Men moved in the camp below. One of them threw wood on the fire and it flared up, setting the cage bars to gleaming. She longed to see her father, who was hidden there, and pounded with her fist on her bloody leg to turn aside an evil thought that he might have died before she could reach him.

There, on the eastern edge of the canyon, the sun moved imperceptibly toward full day. Wind blurred the trees that grew on it, there, to the east, the direction of the fort where Good Plume was to be hanged.

She had heard the soldiers speak of it, how he would hang until his neck gave way and his body stretched almost to the ground, birds stealing his eyes. The soldiers had laughed, saying the birds liked best the soft meat of the groin; they would peck away his manhood. And rats would climb the timber he hung from and run down the chains, eating his flesh. He would be left there for all to see, to jeer at and to hate, a brittle set of bones until the spine fell apart and the arms and legs fell to earth, a part of him dropping away each season, leaving only the high skull at the end of a rusted chain.

When the men did not break camp, it came to her that something unusual had occurred to halt their journey, and she counted them, discovering two were missing.

The sun touched Mr. Bessie's nearly bald head, making it easy to identify him. The white man who gave the orders was there also, and one of the soldiers. She had found the stinking watery dung left by the black man's sickness along the wagon trail and knew he was in the single tent. So there were but four of them, and Jake Moon nowhere to be seen. A blanket lay lumped under a tree; perhaps he slept there, she could not tell.

Three arrows and a bow and a knife. They were enough.

She descended through a rock chimney she found in the cliff, the bow about her neck, the arrows in her teeth. Reaching bottom she hurried into the deep shadows of a birch grove, sliding between the slender trunks, thick as cornstalks in a garden. She made no sound. The ground was soft and moist; the silvery leaves brushed against her face. A lodge-high growth of bushes separated her from the camp.

Through the gnarled branches she saw the rear of the wagon and two horses eating the sparse grass. Hopewell was seated on a stump, pulling on his boots. Bessie stood next to the old riverbed, a pail in his hand. A sour taste rose in her throat.

"Dead water again," Bessie called to Hopewell, who stood up and stamped his feet to settle his boots.

"Try downstream, there's a fairly clear pool there."

"I don't want to go alone," Bessie heard the whine in his own voice and was dismayed. What was happening to him, where was his courage, what had changed him? His thoughts were interrupted by Hopewell, who hobbled over and looked down at the green, murky water. "All right," he said, "I'll go with you."

They carried their rifles, walking warily until a stand of willows took them from sight.

Now! exulted Grass Heart, seizing the moment to step from the thicket to the wagon.

Good Plume stood facing her, a heavy chain running from his neck to his wrists, then to the bars. He looked at her with love. "I smelled you, two nights ago, I knew you were near," he said, working the words around his black tongue. His thin, bare body was splattered with blood; there were holes where a knife had stabbed and pricked at him, and the raw purple of burns speckled his chest and belly. His leg angled off in a new direction where it had been kicked by a booted foot. Pain streaked his face with new wrinkles; his white hair, crusted with blood, crawled with flies.

"Who did this to you?"

"The soldier, it gives him pleasure."

"Where is he?"

"He sleeps there by the tree. He spills my water on the ground, and throws away my food. He is a devil."

Talley saw nothing but her eyes, the flawed one the last thing in his memory when she drew the knife blade across his throat and severed his neck.

Hobie had come to the tent door. He saw her. He saw what she did, saw blood. He did not speak, but gestured to Jake Moon who peered out the flap in time to see the scalp in her fist. He closed the flap on the scene.

Good Plume nodded his splendid skull when she displayed the bloody trophy and his free hand reached up and scratched his earlobe.

"That was good," he said, then stared hard at her through the white fringe across his eyes. "I am dying," he told her.

"Yes. I know."

"Free me, let me go."

She knew what he was asking of her and said, "I can't."

"It is all I ask of you." He spoke truly; another sunset and his spirit would leave his body forever. She had to accept it; he needed death.

↩

HOW WELL HE KNOWS ME! she thought. Her hand was steady, her vision clear. She lifted the bow and tested the string. Fitting the red arrow to it she drew back the cord.

It took him in the breast, the flat thump breaking the silence that held them.

"Another," he told her. "Send this one true."

The twang of the bow sounded and golden feathers grew from his gaunt ribs. He blinked. Then the black arrow struck his heart. It emptied his eyes. He smiled at her.

In the grove she pressed her face to the sweet earth, lying there until voices broke the quiet. She ran to the cleft, climbing swiftly, heedless of her bleeding leg, the useless bow around her neck. Shouts of mingled fear and anger echoed up the hollow column as she gained the ledge, her mind vacant of everything but his final smile.

When the wagon rattled away soon after, she watched them go. Hobie held the reins, with Jake Moon sitting erect beside him. Two horsemen galloped out ahead. The cage lay in the sand, empty, sunlight gilding it.

Once more she went down into the canyon, this time boldly. They had buried the soldier, a spill of sand covering his body. Her father, free of chains, rested against a tree. A blanket was folded beside him. She laid him in it and tied it with the string from the bow. He looked so small in death; it seemed there was scarcely anything left to him, and she laid him in the fork of a tree, securing him with vines and creepers.

When she went to drink from the pool, she shared it with the waterdancers who skimmed atop it, then caught two mice, roasted them in the ashes of the forgotten fire, and ate with a good appetite.

OUT ON THE PRAIRIE, the wagon jerked and squealed. Hobie glanced at Jake Moon and saw that he was weeping.

"You could of stopped her, if you wanted," Hobie said, looking away.

"I didn't want," Jake said.

"You left your good blanket."

Jake stuck out a trembling lip. "I had no deerskin or buffalo robe. I gave him my blanket instead. It was mine to give."

"You knowed her. I kin tell, you knowed her real good," Hobie ventured, still not looking at the man.

"Yes. I know her," and Jake wiped at his cheeks.

"I wouldn't care *a thing* to know that gal, not at all, no sir," said Hobie and gave a nervous shake to the reins. "Git up, horse, move fast."

〜

IN THE EVENING LIGHT, Grass Heart went up to the prairie, turning her face to the west where, beyond the scarlet clouds stretching across the fading sky, the river waited for her.

Far above, in the luminescent sky, swallows darted through the soft air, like children in a game of catch-me. She, too, had played the game of catch-me, far back in a lost time, in childhood. Lifting her voice she cried out: "Catch me if you can, catch me if you will!"

Laughter caught her by the throat and she stopped until her breath returned, the swallows, fleeing from her great shout, wheeling away.

"I am going home," she said in wonder. "Bloody Christ! I am going *home!*" and thought of Kills Ree and his promise to come to her again.

The living earth reached out to her; she walked upon it, feeling its heart speaking to her beneath her bare feet. She felt as majestic as the sunset, as noble as the bravest warrior, as strong and everlasting as the river that watched for her return.

〜

Afterword

WHEN AN EDITOR from the University of New Mexico Press asked me if I would be interested in reviewing a manuscript with an eye to opining whether or not it should be published, I was happy to oblige, but, as I began to read the manuscript of *Grass Heart,* I was flummoxed: the book began unevenly, and, in particular, I found elements of the dialogue improbable. Had I not already agreed to give a report about the book, had, instead, I simply found it while cruising through a book store, I think I would have returned it to the shelf. Certainly, Louis Owens[1] and Gerald Vizenor,[2] among others, have made me aware of the problems faced by any writer, Indian or non-Indian, who confronts the dilemma of authenticity when writing about Indians; I knew how *authenticity* is far too often more a matter of conforming to expectations imposed from outside than it is a matter of historical fact. Too, I was aware of N. Scott Momaday's[3] commonsensical observation that he had read books by non-Indians writing about Indian matters that he had found to be quite good while the inverse had proved true as well. But despite my willingness to step outside any Euramerican perceptions I might have internalized and despite my hope that I could be as focused on the work itself as Scott Momaday and despite my very conscious rejection of essentializing stereotypes, what Owens defines as the [application of] "Euramerican-generated constructions as templates of 'authenticity'" (17), I still found the title character's use of language incredible.[4] After all, how many Plains Indians in the early nineteenth century would be likely to exclaim "Where did that old piss-pot woman go?" (27) or "Bloody Christ!" (6) or "Great bloody Jesus!" (97)? What I had failed to reckon, I learned as I continued reading, was just *how* internalized my perceptions were.

In his fascinating and wonderfully titled book, *Lies My Teacher Told Me,* James Loewen thoughtfully examines the twelve leading textbooks used to teach American history in American high schools. (*Lies My Teacher Told Me* was published in 1995, but, given the speed at which most curriculum committees work, I feel confident that Loewen's findings will remain current for some time to come.)[5] After Loewen reports that "American Indians have been the most lied-about subset of our population" (99), he goes on to note that, "For 325 years, from the first permanent Spanish settlement in 1565 to the end of Sioux and Apache autonomy around 1890, independent Native and European nations coexisted in what is now the United States. The term *frontier* hardly does justice to this [coexistence], for it implies a line or boundary. Contact, not separation, was the rule. . . ." (108). Setting aside for the moment the more and more often heard questions of who is on the margin and who is not and what difference does it make, anyway, it seems to me sensible to suppose that, when not constrained by a centralized government or governments, people in proximity for a number of years will come to share certain characteristics, foremost among which is likely to be a means of communication. What form that communication takes (whether it is a melding like, say, Spanglish, or a dominant language shot through with terms derived from the dominated as, for example, the mutually comprehensible terms like *boocoo* and *hootch* and *number ten* picked up by American soldiers in Vietnam), and why, I'll leave to linguists to explain, but, while Loewen again seems to come to the aid of understanding when he writes that "Native Americans also became well known as linguists, often speaking two European languages (French, English, Dutch, or Spanish) and at least two Indian languages" (104), upon reflection I began to wonder why I looked to him for affirmation of what Walsh had already addressed in an exchange between Good Plume and his daughter, Grass Heart:

"Those words! Where do you get them? . . . Such bad language!"

[Grass Heart] opened her eyes very wide. "From those white men, those friends of yours and the others who visit here."

"Don't use them. Please." (28)

Those words, I have to ask myself, why didn't I believe *them?*

At the very core of *Grass Heart* is a stunning description of the effect of smallpox on an Indian village. Since at first Walsh seems to toy with the disease by having it arrive on a boat named *Saint Peter,* I suppose I might be forgiven for making a trope of "infection" and pointing out how Indian culture was infected by European culture and answering my question by extending the observation to include how the Indian language was infected as well, an excellent example of which is when Good Plume asks his daughter to stop using the language she learned "from white men." But I believe that is too limited. When Walsh points out, "the Indian people had no defenses against the disease" (74), the implications seemed quite clear—until, that is, I recognized one of the templates Owens warns about.

Even a brief glimpse at the history of *Homo sapiens* will reveal a disturbing number of attempts by one people to exterminate another. Among the most effective means to a genocidal end is defined by Richard

Slotkin in *Gunfighter Nation: The Myth of the Frontier in Twentieth-Century America.*[6] He calls this particular tool the "savage war":

> The premise of "savage war" is that ineluctable political and social differences—rooted in some combination of "blood" and culture—make coexistence between primitive natives and civilized [peoples] impossible on any basis other than that of subjugation. . . . resistance to settlement therefore takes the form of a fight for survival; and because of the "savage" and bloodthirsty propensity of the natives, such struggles inevitably become "wars of extermination" in which one side or the other attempts to destroy its enemy root and branch. (12)

The efficacy of such a "savage war" is usually supplemented by a supporting literature that provokes and sanctifies it, which, in the literature of the United States, is perhaps most conspicuously apparent in "dime western" novels and movies of the same ilk. Seen in this light (that is, in light of literature and popular culture acting to justify genocide rather than as *innocent* entertainment), the construction of the U.S. national heritage in terms of a cowboys-and-Indians history is hardly benign, and whether in *The Last of the Mohicans* or *Dances with Wolves* the portrayal of a sad *inevitability* of extinction is anything but innocent. Perhaps Walsh had in mind all along to show how deeply the "infection" might spread. Perhaps she realized that even the best intentioned could be duped by a clever metanarrative. Perhaps she intended us to know that she drew some of the power of her descriptions of smallpox from looking at the scars she saw on herself. There's no way to know. But there are signs as troubling as the first little flu-like symptoms and rash must have been in the time before smallpox had been contained.

That Good Plume knows about smallpox and about "the magic

needle" (74) makes it certain that the author knew there was during the time she was writing about some effective prophylactic against the virus, whether variolation or vaccination. Indeed, Walsh's ability to project herself into a particular time and place is what gives the book its power. But when she notes that "there were but thirty-one families left of the Mandan" (108) and among them only "four young women" (112) *before* the Sioux come, and, when she notes later that "the village was abandoned" (138), our only conclusion can be that now the Mandan are gone, lost to the ravages of disease and inter-tribal war. For all we know as readers, Good Plume is the very last of the Mandan when he says to Grass Heart, "Free me, let me go," which we quickly learn is a euphemism for killing him— and to which Grass Heart responds by thinking, "She has to accept it; he needed death" (158). As if that weren't enough to make us very clear about the Mandan's fate, when at the very end Grass Heart tells us she is going home, she is sure to tell us in such a way that we can conclude *only* that *home* is with the *Cheyenne*. (Since Grass Heart herself is mixed-blood Mandan and Cheyenne, any children she has with her Cheyenne husband, Kills Ree, would be far more Cheyenne than Mandan.) At which point I think it is fair to conclude that Walsh has put neat closure to her novel before the good of the people about whom she has written with such skill, the greatly diminished in number but to this day surviving members of the Mandan.[7]

In *Mixedblood Messages*, Owens warns us that "Just as the oppressively literate modernists felt justified in demanding that readers know a little Greek and Roman mythology as well as the entire literary history of the Western world, Native American writers have begun to expect, even demand, that readers learn something about the mythology and oral histories of Indian America" (10). If writers may reasonably expect a minimum standard of cultural literacy from their readers, I would suggest that readers may demand quite a bit more than the minimum from their writers. By now, I believe, it has been generally accepted that "truth" is relative, which is to say, there is some recognition that truth changes according to the perspective from which it is apprehended and reported. In a recent issue of *Poets & Writers,* Helen Benedict[8] tells us what sort of truth we should look for in a work of fiction: "The subjective truth of what it means to be a human being in the world. . . . not just on the outside, but within: the longings, the moral decisions, the defiance, suffering, pain, and triumphs of the human soul" (46). I would argue that *Grass Heart does* present the sort of truth Benedict so nicely defines; however, the larger question of what we are to do with what Walsh has done to "historical fact," particularly as such rearrangement of the "facts as known" relative to Indians generally undergirds the motive and rationale for over four hundred years of "savage war."

After I had read *Grass Heart* and had begun to consider whether or not I could recommend its publication, I thought first of Ward Churchill's[9] comments about what he found to be the negative impact of two very different movies that he manages to link together seamlessly, *Lawrence of Arabia* and *Dances with Wolves:*

> It's all in the past, so the story goes; regrettable, obviously, but comfortably out of reach. Nothing to be done about it, really. . . . Best that everyone—Euroamericans, at any rate—pay a bit of appropriately maudlin homage "to our heritage," feel better about themselves for possessing such lofty sentiments, and get on with business as usual. (247)

In some ways, it isn't hard to place *Grass Heart* into the *Last-of-the-Mohicans-Dances-with-Wolves-Lawrence-of-Arabia*-comfortably-out-of-reach metanarrative that continues to act in the service of an essentially colonial effort either to obliterate or to acculturate beyond recognition America's First Peoples. On the other hand, we may observe about *Grass Heart* that its Indian characters are fully rendered, thoughtful and self-sufficient, *recognized* human beings and that both the setting and the Indian-white interactions are uncommonly credible, particularly given the time frame of the early nineteenth century. The portrayal of life in the Indian village has about it the feel of what life probably *was* like during that time, neither simplified nor glorified, and the same may be said of the inter-tribal interactions. Which is not even to mention the extraordinary rendering of the smallpox epidemic. In short order, I found myself engaged in an absurdist sort of mathematics in which I was trying not only to assign quantifiable values to various elements of a *novel* but also to subtract some elements and add others according to theorems of my own making—theorems no mathematician could take seriously. Finally, however, three nonmathematical factors combined to get me off the uncomfortable fence I had been sitting.

Both Russell Thornton's[10] *American Indian Holocaust and Survival: A Population History Since 1492* and Nancy Shoemaker's[11] *American Indian Population Recovery* document remarkable growth in American Indian populations during the twentieth century. While there is too much in the history of the United States to allow me to agree with Shoemaker's assertion that "with a current population of two million, [Indians] are no longer at risk of being remembered in history as the 'vanished' Indian" (103), with full awareness of the horrific and inexcusable social and economic inequities that continue to exist for Native Americans, I *am* willing to risk a limited optimism that would allow me to believe that Indians are vanishing less quickly than at any time since Europeans set foot on the American continent. That being the present circumstance, it is then possible to make a case for *Grass Heart* based upon its many positive qualities, only a few of which are mentioned above. The novel *does* work to negate many aspects of the stereotypes[12] so frequently projected upon

Indians, and it does provide dynamic characterizations and imagery that bring to life historians' too often dry and lifeless accounts. In short, so long as its readers are directed to certain caveats, *Grass Heart* offers far too much to allow it to sit unpublished and gathering dust on a shelf. When I made these thoughts known to that same kind editor who had first invited me to review the manuscript, she agreed wholeheartedly and invited me to write this afterword. And in the process of doing so, while carefully reviewing *Grass Heart* and considering my thoughts about it, I had the most gratifying experience of all: at the same time that careful review affirmed the novel's strengths, it also revealed just how much is to be gained from flushing out those seemingly innocuous elements that have made the destructive metanarrative possible. Those elements, like many of the bacteria that cause disease, can only flourish in darkness; exposed to light, they shrivel up and die.

—JAMES COLBERT
Albuquerque
February 2001

Notes

1. Louis Owens is both novelist and scholar. Although not quoted from herein because *Mixedblood Messages* focuses more specifically on issues of Indian identity, his *Other Destinies: Understanding the American Indian Novel* (Norman: University of Oklahoma Press, 1994) offers sophisticated, though accessible, insights into the various thematic elements present in Native American literature.

2. Gerald Vizenor, too, is both novelist and scholar. *Narrative Chance: Postmodern Discourse on Native American Indian Literatures*, edited by Gerald Vizenor (Norman: University of Oklahoma Press, 1993), is strongly theory-based and poses arguments for multiple readings of Native American texts, a brilliant strategy for using postmodern discourse to give the lie to the constructed histories that have stereotyped Indians and to re-vision tribal histories while examining issues of concern to Native American writers such as (among many others) origins, marginality, otherness, and the relation of speech and writing.

3. The novelist and scholar N. Scott Momaday is, arguably, the best known Native American writer. Here, Momaday's observation was recorded by Louis Owens in *This Is about Vision: Interviews with Southwestern Writers*, Crawford, John F., William Balassi, and Annie Eysteroy, editors (Albuquerque: University of New Mexico Press, 1990), 63.

4. Owens, Louis. *Mixedblood Messages: Literature, Film, Family, Place.* Norman: University of Oklahoma Press, 1998.

5. Loewen, James. *Lies My Teacher Told Me: Everything Your American History Textbook Got Wrong.* New York: Simon & Schuster, 1995.

6.   Slotkin, Richard. *Gunfighter Nation: The Myth of the Frontier in Twentieth-Century America.* New York: HarperPerennial, 1992.

7.   Under the Indian Reorganization Act of 1934, the Mandan were joined with the Hidatsa and the Arikara. The "Three Affiliated Tribes" have a current enrollment of over 9,000.

8.   Benedict, Helen. "Fiction vs. Nonfiction: Wherein Lies the Truth?" *Poets & Writers.* September/October 1999.

9.   Churchill, Ward. *Fantasies of the Master Race: Literature, Cinema and the Colonization of American Indians.* Monroe, Maine: Common Courage Press, 1992.

10.   Thornton, Russell. *American Indian Holocaust and Survival: A Population History Since 1492.* Norman: University of Oklahoma Press, 1998.

11.   Shoemaker, Nancy. *American Indian Population Recovery.* Albuquerque: University of New Mexico Press, 1999.

12.   In *Native American Identities: From Stereotype to Archetype in Art and Literature* (Albuquerque: University of New Mexico Press, 1998), Scott B. Vickers answers the question "What constitutes a Stereotype?" by putting "the images that have been projected onto American Indians from the 'outside' . . . into two distinct categories: one 'positive' (that of the Noble Savage) and one 'negative' (that of the Ignoble Savage)." Thereafter, he lists five attributes of the Noble and six attributes of the Ignoble Savage, noting as he does so that these attributes may be mixed and matched "to produce characters of varying degrees of acceptability to the dominant culture" (4) and that he considers any stereotype to be contributory to "dehumanization and deracination."